W9-ARK-032

seven days & seven sins

Also by

PAMELA DITCHOFF

The Mirror of Monsters and Prodigies (1995)

seven days

seven sins

A Novel in Short Stories

PAMELA DITCHOFF

SHAYE AREHEART BOOKS
NEW YORK

This is a work of fiction. Names, characters, places, and incidents either are the product of the author's imagination or are used fictitiously, and any resemblance to actual persons, living or dead, business establishments, events, or locales is entirely coincidental.

Copyright © 2003 by Pamela Ditchoff

All rights reserved. No part of this book may be reproduced or transmitted in any form or by any means, electronic or mechanical, including photocopying, recording, or by any information storage and retrieval system, without permission in writing from the publisher.

Published by Shaye Areheart Books, New York, New York.
Member of the Crown Publishing Group, a division of
Random House, Inc.
www.randomhouse.com

SHAYE AREHEART BOOKS and colophon are trademarks of
Random House, Inc.

Permissions acknowledgments appear on page 227 and are
an extension of the copyright page.

Printed in the United States of America

DESIGN BY LYNNE AMFT

Library of Congress Cataloging-in-Publication Data
Ditchoff, Pamela, 1950–
Seven days & seven sins : a novel in short stories / Pamela Ditchoff.—
1st ed.
1. Girls—Fiction.   2. Neighborhood—Fiction.   3. Deadly sins—Fiction.
I. Title.
PS3554.I839 S48 2003
813'.54—dc21   2002153104

ISBN 0-609-60979-3

10 9 8 7 6 5 4 3 2 1

First Edition

seven days & seven sins

Prologue

*L*ANTERN HILL LANE is a dead-end street on the south side of Lansing. It is a short street with six houses on the east side and six on the west. Beyond the street's end is a small neighborhood park with a baseball diamond and two sets of swings. All but one house was built in the late forties, when postwar production was high at Oldsmobile.

I live at number 10. My name is Angela Mayfair and I'm twelve years old. My father says I am precocious. I have lived on Lantern Hill Lane all of my life. I know everything about this neighborhood, and I know it's the best place for me to be.

The trees lining the street are old maple, elm, and beech that shade the houses and dapple the green lawns with sunshine. My neighbors take care of their lawns and gardens, paint their houses every five years, and shovel snow from the sidewalks. They know each other's names, but they seldom speak beyond a hello and a wave. It's easier to imagine what may be happening behind the windows across the street. It's easier to think that the people inside are living lives as settled as the houses along Lantern Hill Lane. I know better.

Monday's Child
Is Fair of Face

$\mathcal{T}$HE BLEND of circumstances occurs only in April: late afternoon, an hour or so after rain, sunlight nearly white, wet lime-green grass, hyacinth's purple knuckles clenched tight as fists, and no wind at all. Arnie Timmick's pager beeps, usually when he's up a pole repairing storm-damaged lines. The number displayed is his home phone, but he doesn't call his wife. He doesn't because minutes count, and if he is too late, Faye will lock the basement pantry door and stay inside all night.

Arnie drives straight home and finds Faye in the pantry, its small south window casting a light square on her back. She stands before the shelves, hands gripped in her hair, counting cans. Even though there may be only thirty, she counts the same cans over and over in a rush: "Two hundred and five, two hundred and six, two hundred and seven."

Arnie says "I'm here" and moves to a position where she can see him, peripherally because she won't take her eyes from the cans. Faye keeps counting until she reaches 522. Face blotched, breathing rapid, she turns to him, and he can barely stand the seconds before the click of recognition when she cries, "Arnie."

They go upstairs and he draws her a bath, sits on the commode and watches her soak, watches as she slides all the way under, as tiny bubbles rise from her nose. He marvels at the beauty of his wife *(marvel* is the actual word Arnie would use), because Faye is classically beautiful, like Grace Kelly or Audrey Hepburn. That he is a dwarf does not influence his perception. Faye loves him as best she can love, and although she's beautiful enough to be a movie star or a fashion model, she doesn't know it because when she looks in a mirror she sees a face without features.

ARNIE MET Faye three years ago. He was updating the phone system in a psychologists' group office when Faye walked into the reception area. She took his breath away. The dress that swayed about her ankles was pale gray, and she wore no jewelry. Her black hair was braided away from her face, away from her dark blue eyes, and her skin looked as if she had never spent a day in the sun. The full effect made Arnie recall an enameled tin cup from which he drank milk as a child.

Every person that passed through the area stared at Faye. The guy sitting across from her made no pretense of gawking. A pharmaceutical rep was eyeballing her while chatting up the receptionist who cut her eyes in Faye's direction whenever the rep turned his head. Faye was the embodiment of everything that had been out of reach to Arnold Timmick, and he intended to keep her at arm's length. Arnie's history with beautiful girls was generally confined to being the target of mean-spirited remarks. He hated their haughty, self-confident conceit.

However, Faye grew edgy under this scrutiny, biting the inside of her lip, jiggling her foot, checking the wall clock. Arnie thought if she had wings, she'd fly to the ceiling light and bang against it over and over again.

After patching in the final extension, he lifted the receiver and saw that Faye was watching him. Her eyes held his with a silent plea, a reflection of his own past desperation, and Arnie decided to take action.

Impulse is the first thing taunted out of you when you're different, and Arnie was not inclined to act impulsively. He would like to say he acted with dignity—not the antiquated sentiment used to describe the physically or emotionally maimed who stoically shuffle through life without a whimper of discontent, but dignity as a measure of worth, repute, and honor. There's honor in a man willing to risk his pride to take the heat off someone else.

Arnie would not tell you that as he closed his toolbox an image came to mind of the last time he acted impulsively. When Jay Brandstatter wrestled Peter Alexander, the skinny kid who refused to shower after gym, to the locker room floor, Arnie kicked Jay square center in his bulging calf muscle. As Peter grabbed his clothes and ran, Jay stuffed Arnie into a locker and padlocked the door. Two hours passed before Miss Richards, the AV lab instructor, concerned when Arnie didn't show for class, harangued Coach Brownley into checking the locker room.

In the psychologists' office, Faye stopped fidgeting as Arnie walked toward her. Through years of practice, he could gauge a reaction in seconds; if the face didn't give way, the body would. Faye's shoulders dropped slightly and her pupils widened. Arnie hopped up on the chair next to hers, hooked his thumbs around his suspenders and began whistling, "Whistle While You Work." Then he glared at the man seated across from Faye and snapped, "What the hell are you lookin' at?"

The man scrambled out the door, the receptionist shuffled papers on her desk, the rep snapped his briefcase shut and said he would drop by later.

Faye's laughter came from her throat, lips closed, chin raised, eyes shut. Arnie saw the sound flutter in the clavicle basin of her neck. She took a handkerchief from her purse and pressed it to her forehead. Then she said, "I can't stand this place another minute. Would you care to walk me home? My apartment's only three blocks away. I'll fix a lunch. My name is Faye Holliwell."

For a tall woman, she had a girlish voice. From the way she drew out her *a's,* Arnie guessed her roots were Southern. He shifted his eyes to the floor, aware that his answer would be a private crucible. Whatever he said, whatever action he took, he might regret it for years to come, depending on her reaction. The easiest thing would be to give her "the look," the expressionless stare that levels unwanted pity, and walk away.

It would be the safest thing to do; at age thirty-one, Arnie was finally able to lie down at night with a sense of contentment. He no longer dreamt of waking and finding his clothes too small. He had a good job, a house on Lantern Hill Lane in a quiet, safe neighborhood, friends he could watch a game with on the big screen at Trapper's, and enough in the bank to make life easy. And though Arnie had been born with his mother's romantic nature, he'd resigned himself to settle for occasional passion in motel rooms after the bars closed with women who were either drunk, depressed, overly curious, or strange and silent.

Faye did not deserve "the look," and Arnie knew this the moment he saw her. "I have another job in half an hour," he said. "Thanks for the offer, though. Name's Arnie Timmick."

Faye's hand trembled slightly as she extended it, and her fingers were cool in Arnie's hand. "You know, if a bottle of Jack Daniel's could speak, I'll bet it would sound like you," she said.

Arnie smiled; this was one he hadn't heard before. During his teens, he had cultivated a bass voice because as much as he loved his father, he did not want to sound like him. His father's voice reminded Arnie of a small, yappy dog.

When a man exited one of the offices, the receptionist said, "The doctor will see you in five minutes, Faye."

Faye stood abruptly; her handkerchief fluttered to the floor and she was through the door before Arnie could jump down from his chair. The cloth was white and smelled like lily-of-the-valley. Arnie grabbed his toolbox and headed for the elevators.

He caught up with her on the sidewalk out front. She stood with her back to the street, facing the building's reflective glass panels. Arnie was close enough to see the downward turn of her mouth mirrored in the glass.

"You dropped this," he said, holding up the handkerchief.

Faye turned slowly and took the cloth. She shaded her eyes with her left hand. "It is much too bright today."

"That's my company van," Arnie said, pointing to a vehicle with MICHIGAN BELL painted on the side. "Would you like a lift home?"

Arnie opened the door, and as Faye climbed in, a breeze caught her skirt, exposing legs long and white as a field of snow. Walking to the driver's side, he imagined Faye watching him climb the three, custom-built steps, sitting in the seat twice as high as the passenger's, placing his feet on the raised pedals. But she kept her gaze on the street until Arnie started the van and asked: "Where to?"

"Two blocks down Capitol, left on Madison, number 592."

Arnie parked in the drive of a narrow, two-story house, one of those turn-of-the-century downtown buildings renovated for the influx of yuppies during the eighties.

"I can't thank you enough. It's been one of those crazy mornings," Faye said. "How about coming inside for a cold drink?"

Arnie ran his hands along his thighs; it was unusually warm for April, but his sweat was not due to the weather. He wanted her out of the van, out of sight. "Sorry, I'm running late."

Faye cocked her head and sighed. "You think maybe I'm crazy because I was in Dr. K's office, some kind of psycho with bodies of phone company employees buried in my backyard."

"No, I thought you might have dwarfs buried in your backyard." This was a test, a roundabout way of getting rid of her, and Arnie expected her to mumble a quick good-bye and hurry inside.

"I do—six of them: Happy, Grumpy, Sleepy, Sneezy, Doc, and Bashful. That would make you Dopey."

Arnie laughed and shook his head. "Truth is, I have eight calls this afternoon. Maybe another time."

"Saturday night, six o'clock sound okay, Arnie?"

STANDING IN Faye's foyer, watching her bend and slip the back strap of a sandal over her heel, Arnie felt his stomach compress. *Why did I come? What's she up to? Why would a woman with her looks be interested in me?*

She wore red pedal pushers and a cropped T-shirt. Chris Isaak played from the stereo. Arnie wished he had brought something; he'd considered bringing flowers, but he didn't want to give the wrong impression.

"Dinner will be ready soon. Come on back to my office."

Arnie followed Faye down a hallway that was bare of photos, mirrors, or paintings. He stood in the doorway as she sat in front of a computer.

"Only two more entries," she said. A rotund orange cat poked its head out from beneath the desk and rubbed against her ankle.

"What are you working on?" Arnie asked.

"Surveys in zip format, at the moment. I work freelance data entry for dozens of companies. I'm better with letters and numbers than I am with people," Faye said.

Arnie chose not to cross that line. He glanced around the room: a double file cabinet sat next to the desk, which was clear but for the computer and a framed photograph of the cat. There were no posters, plants, or books. The room didn't look lived-in.

A buzzer sounded from the kitchen, causing Faye's body to twitch.

"Want me to turn that off?" Arnie asked.

"Yes, please."

The cat darted in front of him, leading the way to the kitchen, stopping at her empty bowl. Arnie couldn't reach the timer and cursed himself for not thinking about how high it would be before offering to turn the damn thing off. He looked for something to stand on; there were two, fifties soda-fountain-style stools pulled up to a U-shaped counter, two place settings, a pillar candle, and a bottle of red wine. He could push a stool over to the oven, but screw that. Faye came in and snapped off the timer. "I thought you were going to turn it off."

Arnie reached as high as he could, his fingers three inches shy of the timer, then looked at Faye, exasperation clear in the set of his mouth.

Faye's chin puckered. "I don't understand you. I like you, Arnie. One minute you come to my rescue and the next you push me away. Why?"

Arnie shoved his hands into the pockets of his jeans. "I don't know. I'm sorry. Something smells delicious."

Long after the salmon, baked potatoes, and salad were gone, Arnie and Faye remained in the kitchen. Once Arnie got past Faye's looks, he found her easy to talk with, though he did most of the talking. Faye answered his questions briefly, some with merely a shrug. She was born in Marmet, West Virginia, in 1974, left the day after graduation to summer with an Aunt in Lansing and stayed. That was all she offered. However, she was full of questions for Arnie. Was he a happy kid? Did he like school? Who was his favorite teacher? Who was his best friend? How did he get started in the phone business? Where did he live? She listened to him attentively, twisting a lock of hair between her fingers.

If Arnie had not been enjoying himself to such a high degree, he might have realized this was the first time in his memory that a woman seemed to hang on his every word. He was telling her the story of how Fender, his Brittany spaniel, got her name when he noticed the room had grown dark but for the candle's glow.

"I guess I should be going," he said, and turned to Faye. Her lips parted slightly as if to protest, then closed together in a pout. The urge to kiss those lips hit Arnie with unexpected force, followed immediately by the need to flee. He placed his foot on the top rung of the stool, preparing to step down. Before he could, Faye blew out the candle and pressed her mouth to his.

ARNIE RESISTED loving Faye. Besides the obvious differences, something felt slightly off, like the nagging suspicion that you'd left a burner on and would go home to find your house in flames. Yet he had dreamed of Faye in those moments before sleep when memories and possibilities blur. He had not envisioned a face or a figure, but rather a combination of qualities: spontaneity, easy laughter, unconditional faith in him, and the natural curiosity that compliments intelligence. Faye had all these qualities and some Arnie could not have imagined he would find endearing, like the way she slept curled in a ball with both hands tucked between her knees.

By June, Arnie's resistance was giving way and would have completely vanished if not for the fact that their time together was spent entirely at either her house or his. Faye didn't like restaurants because "You never know what they're up to in the kitchen." Theaters made her claustrophobic, people jammed together and talking in the row behind you. Each time he suggested an outing, she would drop her chin and say, "I'd rather have you all to myself."

At first those words would quicken Arnie's pulse and precipitate an erection. However, in the daytime working hours, a suspicion that Faye was using this as an excuse not to be seen with him began eating at Arnie. So one early July evening when Faye dipped her chin and spoke those words, he said, "You're embarrassed to be seen with me."

Faye's arms flew up, reminding Arnie of black-and-white westerns when somebody says "Hands up."

"No, no—Arnie, it's not you—it's me. I hate that people stare at me, the ones that know . . . that can see through me," she stammered.

"Faye, people stare because you're beautiful."

"Don't say that. Pretty is as . . ." Faye trailed off and bit her lip. *"You're* beautiful, Arnie; you are perfectly beautiful."

She wrung her hands as if trying to squeeze the right words out, the words that would erase the lines of accusation drawn in his face. "When I'm with you," she said, "I feel weightless, like swinging high, high as I can go."

FAYE CONTINUED to see Dr. K through that summer. Arnie didn't ask her about it, and to his relief, she never raised the subject. Not that he didn't care about Faye's emotional well-being, but whatever was being discussed in the office of Dr. K didn't appear to have an affect on their relationship. Besides, Arnie had no use for the profession. He considered psychologists scab pickers with a stockpile of psycho bandages, like pinching a baby to make him cry, then hugging him to your chest and cooing in his ear.

This opinion stemmed from Arnie's single encounter with a family therapist when he was sixteen. His mother merely raised an eyebrow when Arnie bought a red leather jacket from the boy's department at Hudson's. She didn't object to the black boots or the choke collar with studs. But when he came to dinner one night with a swastika inked on the back of his hand, she demanded he go wash it away. Arnie sneered and mumbled, "It doesn't mean anything."

His mother rapped her knife against the table. "Arnold, it's a sign of evil. Jews were not the only ones Hitler exterminated. Ten thousand dwarfs died under that sign, that doesn't mean anything to you? One of them was your great-grandpa."

Arnie's father wept into his napkin, and Arnie detested him for it. He shoved himself away from the table, shouting, "Why did you have me? What were you thinking? Fifty-fifty the kid won't be a freak?"

A week later, at Riven Center, it was his mother's turn to cry. After she explained her concerns, the therapist began grilling her: Why had she not sought therapy earlier for a special-needs child? Why wasn't the father present? Did you discuss the possibility of raising a dwarf before becoming pregnant? Had his condition influenced her discipline or lack thereof? Had she breast-fed him?

That's when Arnie reached up, grabbed the guy's tie and yanked his head downward. "Shut your stupid mouth, asshole," he growled, his face an inch from the therapist's. The fear Arnie saw in his face was almost worth his mother's tears.

ARNIE PROPOSED to Faye in December. Approaching her front door, he was struck by how sharply defined everything seemed to be: three shades of gray in the low slung clouds, the pines intensely green against them; his breath exhaled in white puffs; the thin layer of ice crunching beneath his boots; a cobweb on Faye's porch, torn and dangling with the weight of a few snowflakes; the feel of the blue velvet box in his pocket.

Arnie did not analyze his reasons for choosing the engagement ring without Faye's knowledge. However, in the back of his brain the reasons added up: Faye's reluctance to venture out; the possibility of an embarrassed clerk, fumbling to be polite to a man who couldn't see over the counter; and the advantage of surprise. By presenting a glittering diamond set in an antique gold band, he would not need to propose; he would simply give Faye the box and hold his breath.

Arnie couldn't breathe as they sat on the couch and she opened the box. He watched the play of emotions on her face: astonishment to tenderness to tears.

"I love you, Arnie, and I want to be your wife, but . . ."

Arnie's mouth went dry and his heart skipped a beat. She

was about to break it off, and he loved her now, loved her more than he could possibly get over. He felt himself growing smaller, sinking into the couch, the orange cat perched on the arm flipping her tail back and forth.

Faye bit her lip and stared at the floor. "Dr. K says I have to be honest with you, Arnie, and tell you that while I appreciate your wit, intelligence, and character . . . it's your size that's most appealing to me."

Arnie laughed, laughed out his surprised relief, set the box on the coffee table laughing, took Faye's hands in his. "And the problem is?"

Faye didn't break a smile. She told him she'd been going to Dr. K for three years. Every April since she was ten years old, she'd been incapacitated by fear and dread—not depression, but panic, so severe on certain days that her skin seemed to dissolve, leaving tissue and bone exposed to every breeze, every sound, every eye. The only possible comfort was submersion in a tub full of water. Until Dr. K persuaded her to try hypnosis, she had no memories to explain why this happened year after year.

Faye said to Arnie: "You're the size I was before my father's brother hurt me when I came home from school . . . after the rain stopped and I went outside. 'Don't scream, don't make a sound or I'll kill you' . . . pulled me through wet grass toward the root cellar . . . pulled me past where hyacinths bloomed, the stump of a purple-green cluster bled white between my fingers . . . dragged me down the steps to where rows of tomatoes and peaches stared out from behind glass, his hands gripped in my hair holding me still. 'You're pretty, so pretty' . . . the air so still my counting sounded like screaming . . . a square of sun from the doorway red against my eyelids, counting, counting even as he ran away . . . then a long shadow, opening my eyes and Father there . . . 'Jesus Christ Almighty,' like a curse. 'What have you done?' . . . holding out my arms and the door closing, the padlock clicked, 'Pretty is as pretty does' . . . the rest of the day and all through the night and the next, my legs sticky with blood, throbbing pain . . . then I was in a bathtub; I guess my mother carried me there, I don't remember. I do remember slipping all the way under the warm water and wanting to stay there forever."

Arnie couldn't speak, his throat choked with grief and rage.

"I'm not going to see Dr. K anymore," Faye said. "He says I'm being dishonest with you and with myself, that I am incapable of a mature, loving relationship until I come to terms with my past. He says my feelings for you are an association with a time when I felt safe. Even if that's true, is it wrong, Arnie? Is that so bad?"

ARNIE CAN'T wait any longer. He dips his hand into the water and touches the top of Faye's head. She surfaces and smiles shyly. "Hi, sweetie."

He gets a towel from the linen closet as Faye rises from the tub, her glistening white curves and fullness making Arnie dizzy with desire even after three years of marriage.

He doesn't regret kissing her that December day after her confession when she asked: "Do you still want to marry me?" Despite the coppery taste at the back of his tongue, knowing

Faye perceived him as childlike, the thing most repugnant to any dwarf, what choice did he have? The alternative was losing her. If he rejected Faye after she had confessed her secrets, the harm would be irreparable.

Arnold Timmick has a good job, a house in a safe, quiet neighborhood, friends to watch Monday night football with at Trapper's, enough money in the bank to make life easy, and a beautiful girl waiting for him at the end of the day. And that's not so bad.

Envy

The First Sin
Envy

*W*HILE MISTING her *Aspasia,* Cora Ladinsky sees Arnie hurry into his house next door. April love, she supposes. He's left work early to make love to his wife. Faye will be wearing the white dress with a blue belt, putting a casserole in the oven, her long hair clipped up. Arnie will come from behind and slide his hands around her thighs. That's how it will start.

Cora wishes he were coming home to her. It's not that she's jealous of Faye; Faye is gorgeous, and Cora knows herself to be homely. She simply wishes there were a special man in her life.

She sniffs the white orchid, a present from her brother a year ago last Christmas and whispers: "Tell me." The scent reminds her of candy wax lips. After the florist delivered the orchid, Cora removed the silver paper and stared at the complex, delicate blossoms. Somehow it seemed the plant was holding a secret meant just for her. She touched the purple spotted labellum of one flower, exposing the anther cap and golden throat, and she blushed from neck to forehead.

Since then she has bought five more plants. They thrive on

the cherrywood stand that held Grandma Euphemia's collection of miniature glass shoes. It's a myth that orchids are hard to grow. Cora appreciates this and tends them lovingly nonetheless. Some species, she once read in a magazine, have developed scents that mimic pheromones to attract a pollinator. Cora does not have the knack for attracting men, and she feels this acutely in the spring.

She sprays *Encyclia cocheeata* last, her black orchid. She had been briefly disappointed when, after receiving the plant from a mail-order nursery, she soon discovered its blooms were greenish-yellow. But the lip was irresistible, marked with three velvety black ridges.

Cora stores the mister under the sink then opens a can of tuna to make a sandwich she'll eat on her 10:00 P.M. break. Squeezing oil out with the lid, she glances up and sees Faye and Arnie's bathroom window cloud with steam.

CORA IS SEATED at her workstation by 5:50, one among hundreds of employees at Lansing's central mail processing center. Betty waves from four stations over. In the ten years she's worked here, Cora has made few friends, and Betty's the only one who hasn't moved into another department or into marriage. Cora owns up to being shy, but she also has come to understand it's not easy to make friends here. She compares this phenomenon to shopping. Her favorite store, Kali's Cottons, has two walls of clothing divided into dresses and skirts, blouses and sweaters, slacks, and accessories. Once, when she rode to the Novi mall with Betty, she came home empty-handed, unable to make a decision, overwhelmed by the number of possibilities. She returns Betty's wave and jots a note: *Bob's Big Boy?*

Normally, Cora wouldn't ask, going to Bob's is a Thursday night tradition. Now and then Betty begs off because she has a date, and Cora usually doesn't mind. Being with Betty is sometimes lonelier than being alone: mostly Betty talks, and Cora listens to either her endless commentary on men or to the number of ways Cora could enhance her appearance. However, Cora wants company tonight. She hands the note over the top of her wall divider and starts sorting the first bin.

The note comes back a moment later: *I have a date with Larry!* Betty's peering over the top of her divider, waiting for Cora's reaction, and Cora can picture her there but can't bring herself to rise from the chair.

By break time Cora has sorted three Incoming bins, separated letters, priority mail, magazines, newspapers, and rewrapped two damaged packages. She enjoys her work and the responsibility of her role in a U.S. government institution. With each empty bin, she experiences a sense of accomplishment and a twinge of patriotism.

"Over here, Cora," Betty hollers from a corner table in the break room. She's sitting with a guy Cora recognizes as an OCR operator. "Cora, you know Larry?"

Larry nods. "Have a seat."

Cora feels a blush coming and quickly says, "Thanks, but I want to read the classifieds."

Cora is still amazed when fabrications fly out of her mouth, a defense she developed as a teenager to avoid embarrassment, which sometimes backfires when she's pressed for details.

"What are you looking for?" Betty asks, and Cora could slap her. Betty knows she's shy, especially around men, and if Betty could just once use her brain for thinking beyond hooking a husband, well, she would certainly appreciate it. Most likely one of those books Betty collects advised: *Show interest in a friend in the presence of your prey,* right below *Don't stare at him* and *Don't dominate the conversation,* which is probably why Betty has gone through so many prospective husbands.

"A greenhouse for my orchids."

As she's walking away, she hears Betty say, "My, yes, she has dozens of them, it's her hobby. You have any hobbies, Larry?"

Cora locates a table with a *State Journal* and sits with her back to the wall. She opens the paper, takes a pencil from her pocket, and writes in the margin:

REASONS I'M LONELY/ALONE

1. Raised on a farm
2. No sisters
3. No close girlfriends after grade school
4. Shy
5. Body shape
6. Uninformed on current fashion, makeup, hairstyles

She can't do a thing about the first three, and she's skeptical about the others. Her shyness came on at puberty, when the girls at school started competing for the boys' attentions, and it's been with her since.

Cora remembers when Betty got a Richard Simmons workout tape after reading about "waist to hip ratio" and the magic number that draws men's attention. Cora has never bothered to measure, but she guesses her waist is about an inch smaller than her hips and her bust about an inch larger.

She pictures the contents of her clothes closet, slim pickin's. Cora doesn't follow fashion trends, nor does she read fashion magazines; nobody in them looks like her.

Betty laughs, a sound like wind chimes, and Cora looks up from her list. Betty isn't one bit prettier than I am, she thinks, but damn, how she's changed. It's as if she was a plain old pumpkin that up and got carved, someone stuck a candle inside, and now her face is lit up like a jack-o'-lantern.

Cora Ladinsky can't transform herself in this manner, in spite of her longing for love. Frowning, she draws a large X through her list, and the word *orchid* catches her eye. Under the "Meetings" subheading of Community Calendar, she reads:

Greater Lansing Orchid Society: *Meets each second Tuesday of the month, 6:00 P.M., Natural Science Bldg., Room 8, Michigan State University.*
All orchideliriumites welcome. For more information call 517.333.7543

Cora rips the page free, folds it into a square, and drops it in her lunch box.

CORA PARKS her Saturn in the driveway and studies her house. With the Grow Light shining on her orchids, she's reminded of a picture from an old storybook: a cozy cabin in the midst of deep dark woods. Of course, at this hour it's the only window lit on the block, and it's not a cottage, it's Grandma Euphemia's house on Lantern Hill Lane, given to Cora as a hedge against her dubious future.

How many years ago was it? Twelve? She heard her parents' voices floating through the floor register after Grandma's funeral.

"I'm giving the house to Cora."

"Whatever for? She don't need your mother's house. Louie?"

"I know she don't need it, but I want to give it to her."

"I thought we settled on selling the place. I got that new freezer picked out."

"Kate, she's twenty. What's going to happen for her around here?"

"Well, didn't she mention some community college?"

"Seen any application papers?"

"I guess not, but what's she need with Euphemia's house? You expect her to move in there, don't you? Lou, she's a lot of help to us on the farm, and I'd miss her. She'd have to get a job in Lansing. She should stay here. She'll meet someone . . . now, don't you look at me like that. I was a late bloomer too."

"Fred and Joe Williams had their eyes on you when you was just fourteen. Most women get a—a bloom around sixteen or so. When she's got that, she don't need anything else, and if she don't have it, don't matter much what else she's got. Cora don't have that bloom, but she can have property."

Cora leaves her lunch box in the hall and drops to the couch with a grunt. She picks up a catalog from yesterday's mail, flips to the order form and writes in the names of the orchids she check-marked earlier: *Brassia caudata,* the spider orchid; *Epidendrum atropurpureum,* the spice orchid; *Bulbophyllum medusae,* the Medusa head orchid. The total bill is shocking, but Cora's shock momentarily gives way to the same guilty satisfaction she experiences when eating a hot fudge sundae.

Cora crosses the room to smell the blossoms, a nightly ritual she equates with aromatherapy. She leans forward and sniffs deeply. Her eyes pool with tears and she says: "Help me to bloom; tell me your secrets."

She stares at each plant, half believing the floral lips will quiver and an answer will come out of the brightly colored throats. A few minutes pass before Cora realizes she's tired to the bone. She yawns expansively over her orchids, then chokes as her mouth tingles with a burst of musk and bitter almond. Her field of vision explodes in brilliant orange turning to deep purple, and her knees buckle.

CORA GROANS, squinting in the bright sunlight. She runs her tongue over her lips and tastes something rusty, like the smell of moldering hay. A weight presses against her chest.

"Oh, Lordy," she cries, and raises her head. She's in a supine position, arms and legs stretched as if making a snow angel. She sees the *Aspasia* below her right foot and the *Encyclia cocheeata* below her left. The *Stanhopea* touches her right hand and the *Maxillaria* is near her left. And there, as if she had given birth, is the *Cymbidium,* upright and blooming between her thighs. Soil, bark, and perlite litter the floor, but the plants are not uprooted nor wilted. However, one appears to be missing. Cora cautiously tips the table off her chest, sits up, and finds the *Vanda multiflora* sitting just above where her head had been. She lifts the *Cymbidium* from between her legs and gingerly stands. Her whole body aches the way it did when she had the Asian flu . . . What's this? Cora gapes at the floor with the realization that if she drew a line connecting the plants, a star would be formed.

Only after her orchids are seen to, soil replaced and misted from the petals, the table cleaned and polished, the carpet vacuumed, does Cora tend to herself. In the small, yellow and gray tiled bathroom she reaches for the medicine cabinet and stops short at her reflection. A grape-sized bump protrudes from her forehead, and her lower lip is swollen and streaked with blood. She swallows two aspirin and turns on the shower.

After undressing, she discovers a slash bruise on her collarbone and smaller ones on her right arm and left shin. She's never fainted, why last night? The answer has something to do with the orchids, and that's a little scary and thrilling at the same time, like the moment preceding a first kiss.

WEARING HER chenille robe and slippers, Cora shuffles stiffly to the front door. She opens it to get the morning paper and sees Arnie kiss Faye good-bye before climbing into his company van.

Lordy, I'm supposed to work tonight. She pictures people staring at her bruises, sniffing around like bloodhounds on raccoon scent.

It's a beautiful, washed-out blue, Michigan spring morning. A westerly breeze carries the fragrance of Grandma Euphemia's hyacinth beds inside. After breakfast she'll call her supervisor and take a few days off. Cora has foregone too many sick days in the past ten years to count. Surely the swelling will be gone by Wednesday.

Cora leaves the newspaper on the porch, bends with a groan to pick up her lunch box, and goes to the kitchen. Opening the box, she sees the page she tore from the *State Journal* last night. She smooths it out on the table and fixes a bowl of cereal. This morning the meeting does not have the same appeal as it did in the break room watching Betty flirt. Cora tells herself it's because the group meets at MSU and she dislikes driving there. She knows her way to the Wharton Center, where she's seen *Cats, Phantom,* and *Lord of the Dance;* it's easy to get to and easy to park. However, driving the one-way, circling streets winding through most of the campus is a nightmare. The real reason, and she knows this to be true, is she's afraid the club members will be university types, people who speak a language she hasn't mastered.

Her cheeks flush at the thought, and she crumples the paper into a ball. She goes to the living room and gets the catalog order form from the couch. Forget the few bucks I'll save by regular mail, Cora thinks. She picks up the receiver and dials the 800 number.

AT NOON on Tuesday, Cora is deeply asleep, snoring with her mouth open, a wet spot on her pillow. She's walking through a field of orchids large as the maples on Lantern Hill

Lane. The blooms sway high above her, nodding their heads together in conversation. Cora stands on tiptoe trying to hear them, needing to learn their secrets. She begins to climb the stem of a *Cymbidium* when the huge orchid head turns downward, opens its bright lips, and screams the same three words over and over in a language Cora can't understand. She jolts upright, nearly knocking the ringing phone off its cradle.

"Cora? Heard you're sick."

"I'm not sick, Betty. I was washing windows and fell off the stepladder. Nothing's broken, but I bruised myself right and proper. Felt so stupid, didn't want to explain all over the place, so I took some sick time."

There they go again, lies flying out of her mouth. However, in this instance, Cora feels justified. She can't tell Betty what really happened because she doesn't know herself. To add to the mystery, although the swelling has gone down and the bruises have faded, there are three purple vertical lines on her bottom lip that, rather than fading, have grown brighter.

"Cora, I swear, you're the only person I know who would use sick days for spring cleaning."

"I wasn't—"

"Glad to hear it's nothing serious, and speaking of serious, Larry and I went out Saturday night. Let me tell you, we both had a prit-tee good time. I wore my black pants and pink sweater; you know the one I mean, that evens out my skin tones. First we went to Amelio's for dinner, then—"

"Betty, someone's at the door."

"Should I call you back? Never mind—I'll tell you all about it tomorrow night."

Cora throws on her robe and hurries to answer the door. A UPS man stands on the stoop holding a box that reads DO NOT TIP, SPECIAL HANDLING. "I need your signature," he says curtly, extending a clipboard.

He's handsome, extremely so, and Cora realizes she must look a fright. She opens the screen door and is seized by a blush she can feel radiate through the flannel of her pj's. She takes the pen and dashes off a signature.

"Mind if I ask what's in the box?" the man asks.

"Orchids," Cora answers, and reaches for the package, eager to get back inside.

The man keeps the box tucked under his arm. "Is that what smells so good or is it you?" The abrupt change in his tone from clipped and informal to slow and husky causes Cora to blush even more.

"Probably the hyacinth bed there."

He breathes in deeply, closes his eyes, and his jaw muscles flex like two miniature hearts. He wears the expression of a man who is struggling to restrain himself, Cora thinks, and the back of her neck prickles.

"My orchids, please?"

He passes the box to Cora, saying, "I'm off at five. We should get together later."

"I work nights," Cora blurts, and shuts the door. A moment later she peers out the front window from the cover of her orchids. The man throws his cap in the truck, looks back at the house, scratches his head, then drives away.

Why on earth did I slam the door? Isn't that what I've been longing for? Despite her inexperience, Cora could sense that his invitation wasn't special; it was nothing but urgent.

THERE ARE four books on orchids at Between the Lines. Because of her fainting spell on Thursday night and the growing suspicion that the UPS man's attention had something to do with the orchids, Cora has decided to attend the orchid society meeting after all. She chooses *The Orchid Encyclopedia* and pays for her purchase.

Inside her car, Cora tilts the rearview mirror and reapplies her lipstick. She's not one for gazing in the looking glass, but she takes a moment because the lip color seems to have made her dark eyes brighter. She removes the scrunchy from her hair and shakes her head. Gone is the springy copper-colored frizz, replaced by flowing waves worthy of a shampoo ad, bright as a new penny. *This may be a face in bloom. What sort of magic did my orchids work?*

The dash clock reads 4:00, plenty of time to stop at Mike's Market, eat dinner, and dress for the meeting.

A HIGH SCHOOL boy, TODD on his plastic name tag, carries out three bags while Cora cradles a bottle of crangrape juice. He had yanked the bags off the end of the checkout in a manner that led Cora to suspect he's cruel to animals. In her haste to open the trunk quickly and not further antagonize him, the bottle slips from Cora's grip and smashes on the pavement.

"Ah, shit." Todd drops her bags in the trunk and turns his

head sharply away. Cora's cheeks are scarlet as she kneels and begins gathering the broken glass.

"Lady, you're kneeling in the juice and you're gonna cut—"

Cora begins to cry.

"Ah, shit. Lady, I'm supposed to do that. I'm gonna get a broom, so drop those pieces and get up, please, before the manager sees me?"

The desperation in his voice makes Cora stop, and Todd helps her to her feet. She's eye-to-eye with the kid, and a dopey grin spreads over his face.

"Sorry. I'm a real jerk sometimes." He closes the trunk and lifts a corner of his Mike's Market apron to Cora's cheek.

She bats it away as if it were a bug trying to fly up her nose. "I'm okay."

"You still seem kinda shook."

"Really, I'm fine," Cora replies. She opens the car door, and as she's getting inside, Todd opens the passenger door and slides onto the seat. Too astounded to be shy, Cora shouts, "Get out."

"I can't."

Cora follows Todd's downward glance and sees his weenie waving beneath his khakis. He makes a lunge for her and she leaps from the car. Safely back inside the store, Cora waits for her heart to stop drumming then looks out the window. Todd's still in the front seat, head thrown back, hand pumping.

Twenty minutes pass with Cora hovering near the window before the manager asks if there's a problem. Cora can't answer; she simply points to her Saturn.

By the time Todd is yanked from the car, stripped of his apron, and escorted to his ten-speed, it's 4:45. Cora isn't at all sure she'll make the meeting and she would rather not go than walk in late.

CORA HOLDS the orchid encyclopedia to her chest like a shield as she enters Room 8 of the Natural Science Building. She chooses a seat in the last row and surveys the room. There's a dais at the front and a large screen hangs from the ceiling. A woman is stacking papers on a table that also holds an orchid, and oh, Lordy, it's a beaut, a strawberry and cream striped wonder. She begins flipping through her book, hoping to learn the orchid's name before the meeting begins. She ignores the printed descriptions, focusing instead on the photos of brightly colored blooms.

However, there are hundreds of photos and Cora can't wait. *Shyness, be damned, I'm going up there and find out if it's for sale.* Before she can reach the woman who seems to be in charge, a female chorus rings from the back of the room: "Evening, Leslie."

The woman answers, "Evening, girls," and strides past Cora with her nose stuck up in the air. Cora takes a newsletter from the table and starts reading, ignoring the buzz from the back. *Glory be, the orchid's being raffled tonight.* She lays a five dollar bill on the table, tears off five tickets, and returns to her seat.

By 8:10, when Leslie calls the meeting to order, there are sixteen women present and three men. Leslie says she'll hurry through the announcements due to everyone's anticipation of tonight's special event. She announces the need for volunteers for the upcoming Michigan Orchid Growers' Festival, the memorabilia committee, the silent auction committee, and the summer picnic planning committee.

"Now, with distinct pleasure, I turn the floor over to Mr. Bill Cavendish." Leslie's gestures remind Cora of the flair with which Vanna White turns over four vowels. Cora's attention wanders back to the encyclopedia and her search for the strawberries and cream orchid.

She barely notices as Bill sets up a slide projector in the center of the aisle. Someone dashes over to the light switch and holds her hand in midair. "Before I begin the slide show," Bill says, "I wish to extend a warm welcome to our guest. Lights, please."

Cora's head jerks from the book a moment too late, the room has already darkened and the wall screen is lit with the profuse greens of a Florida swamp.

"This is Fakahatchee," Bill says.

The word sounds magical to Cora, like *abracadabra* or *alacazam*. She wishes she could get a better gander at Bill, but she takes in what she can. His back half is in silhouette. He has a bushy head of dark hair, and though he's pear-shaped, he has excellent posture, spine erect, feet apart.

"As you know, Fakahatchee is one of the richest orchid sites in the country," Bill says. "I searched the swamp for days before discovering this tree."

With a click of the projector, a single tree appears, and at first Cora thinks it's infested with some Southern type of white moss. A second click and the girls *Oooh*.

"*Polyrrhiza lindenii*—the ghost orchid."

Cora rises from her seat and walks, trancelike, closer to the screen, where leafless, milk-white blooms spread over brown bark, and the pale green roots form star patterns. Click three fills the screen with a single blossom, six feet high, a slight hint of green in the petal tips, anther cap round and yellow as a yolk, and the lip... *Oh my.*

"Can you see the woman of my dreams?" Bill's voice is barely above a whisper, meant for Cora only. She realizes she is standing beside him, but she can't take her eyes from the screen. And she understands his question, she had seen it immediately: the orchid's lip resembles the head of a woman, hair flipped on either side, slender neck connecting two alabaster arms outstretched, beckoning.

"It's the most beautiful thing I've ever seen." Cora covers her mouth and sniffles. For a moment she believes she can smell the orchid, an intoxicating scent. She breathes deeply, and an image flashes before her eyes: Bill and she together in Fakahatchee, naked white skin on a green moss bed, limbs entwined, a bower of ghost orchids overhead.

Then the scent is gone, leaving Cora flushed, a film of perspiration on her forehead, the ridges on her lip throbbing. She drops into the nearest seat, gripping the arms, wishing she could crawl under it. The two men seated in the front row slowly turn their heads toward Cora, like compass needles gravitating to true North.

She's considering how to leave quietly when a hand comes to rest upon her wrist and taps twice, a comforting touch. Cora gazes up at Bill, and although he keeps his face forward, she can see an impish half smile. He runs through the remaining slides, his commentary on the ghost orchid being endangered and Fakahatchee the only place in the world it can be found sounding to Cora's ears as if she's underwater.

Someone flicks on the lights, and before Leslie can reach the dais to begin the raffle, the two men are out of their seats headed for Cora. They wear the determined-to-get-there-first expression of her father's shoats after he's slopped the trough. Cora presses her spine into the seat's back, steeling herself for a confrontation.

A firm grasp lifts her from the chair; now an arm around her waist is sweeping her down the aisle and out the door. When Cora comes to her senses and digs in her heels, that exquisite, pulse-pounding scent hits her again. If Bill's arm were not wrapped about her waist, she believes she would swoon. They are standing in a circle of amber light cast from a nearby street lamp, and Cora can see him clearly. He is more handsome than the UPS man, more handsome than Betty's Larry, more handsome than any movie star. His eyes are the green of spring and they tenderly hold Cora's reflection; in them, she sees herself as beautiful as an orchid blossom afloat in a clear glass bowl.

"You can learn to control it; I have, and I can teach you how."

Bill's face draws nearer, eclipsing the light, and just before closing her eyes in that scary, thrilling moment preceding a first kiss, Cora sees three velvety black ridges bloom upon his lip.

Tuesday's Child
Is Full of Grace

G RACE IS ABOUT to rediscover the pleasures of being quadrupedal at 11:00 P.M. one Thursday in June while digging a hair ball out from under the fridge. Buddy died last winter, and seeing his dusty black fur had made her fingers ache with the memory of his head beneath her hand.

When she gets down on all fours and crooks a finger around the hair, a pop sounds between her shoulder blades. She freezes in anticipation of pain that does not arrive. Moreover, she feels a loosening in her back accompanied by tingling through her hands. However, as soon as Grace stands, her muscles clench together in spasms. She sinks to her knees, presses her palms against the floor, and the pain subsides. Slowly, Grace allows her spine to curve downward; the motion stretches her belly and pulls tension away from her hips and into her thighs.

After a moment she eases her bottom onto the floor. Buddy's hair has been sucked back under the fridge and Grace swallows to relieve the tightening of her throat. She doesn't want to cry, but she feels utterly lonesome.

She raises her hands close to her face; they're mottled red and white, knuckles slightly swollen.

"Ugly lumps," she mutters, and considers the years she never gave a thought to her hands, dumb servants in a crowded house. She traces the large M on her right palm, playing the memories etched there like grooves in a record: the gold slipped on her finger, learning the map of Roger's body in the darkened bedroom upstairs, the births of three children, oily baby seals, briny with birth scent, lifted to her breast.

Grace laces her fingers together and sighs; fingers that tied shoelaces, braided hair, tucked in shirttails, tugged on boots and mittens, ironed shirts, wrote checks, prepared thousands of meals, and scraped plaque from thousands of teeth.

The children moved away from her in straight lines once she released her grip on the handlebars, handed over car keys, heard their laughter diminish down the road. Four months after Grace's surgery, shortly after their youngest left for university, Roger bought a Harley Electra-Glide and headed for Alaska.

Grace resumes a quadruped position and ambles toward the living room, aware of how natural this movement feels, shoulders rotating in harmony with her hips, ribs expanding and contracting like an accordion. She stops at the coffee table and lies on her back, knees drawn up. A nose print on the table glass reminds Grace that her housekeeping hasn't been as thorough as in years past, but how could she have cleaned that tabletop once a week and not noticed Buddy's signature underneath? She pictures the prescription for bifocals in her desk drawer, then pulls a catalog from the tabletop. She flips through the pages and pauses at an advertisement for the

Master 400 ultrasonic scaler: CLEANS TEETH WITH 32,000 STRAIGHT LINE OSCILLATIONS PER SECOND.

Grace touches the horseshoe scar on the underside of her right forearm and thinks about the dental hygienists who will benefit from ultrasonic technology, who won't feel the numbness begin in the thumb and first two fingers, the hand and arm becoming so painful that sleep is fitful, and even after surgery, the muscles and cartilage failing under pressure. Carpal tunnel syndrome: the condition that took the gleaming, slender, balanced instruments out of her hands.

A noise from the back porch prompts Grace to drop the magazine and crawl to the screen door. She cautiously raises her head and peers into the summer night. A white wicker table is the only object she can see, lying on the concrete sideways. She reaches up and flips on the porch light, remembering the green pear she had left on the table to ripen. She sees only a flash of fur disappearing into the darkness.

BEFORE SHE is fully awake, Grace slides her hand to the other side of the bed. Roger has been gone for eighteen months; his smooth shoulder was the first thing her fingers touched every morning for twenty-three years. For the last five of those years, he would turn off the alarm and get out of bed without a word, leaving her as hollow as the sound of the back door thumping shut. She had stopped loving him long before he left, and now she doesn't miss him as much as she misses the feel of his skin.

Grace sits up and runs her fingers through her short dark

hair. She pulls on the T-shirt she had worn the night before and walks to the stairs. Standing erect, she feels protracted, vulnerable with belly and chest exposed. Pain throbs an inch above her coccyx and she drops to all fours.

Impossible to go hands first, she thinks, then visualizes her toddlers at the top of these stairs, ingeniously trusting their padded backsides to open space. As Grace crawls backward down the stairs, she notices tooth marks on the fourth rung of the banister, a speck of silver glitter in the corner of the seventh step, a bit of Milk Bone biscuit on the tenth.

Grace crawls to the washroom, purposely avoiding eye contact with the kitchen. Mornings once were her best time: dressed in her clean, white hygienist uniform sitting at the kitchen table with a mug of coffee and the newspaper, the mug warm between her hands, newsprint inking her fingertips. She would scratch Buddy's ears and look out the window at her gardens: in spring, tiger crocuses, lily-of-the-valley, tulips, and daffodils. In May she'd plant flats of pansies, alyssum, and petunias to compliment the tulips, peony bushes, Dutch iris, and tea roses.

She gave up caffeine to give up the headaches, gave up newsprint in protest of bifocals, and gave up gardening to the pain in her arm. However, she's not thinking about her losses this morning. Grace is forming the idea that this may be an adventure, a challenge, really, to test the limits of quadrupedality.

She turns on the shower, pulls off her shirt, and climbs into the tub, sitting cross-legged on the starfish bath appliqués. Due to the distance of the showerhead, the spray patters against her skull, stinging her skin. She closes her eyes and imagines herself in a primeval lagoon: waterfalls cascade basso profundo

into emerald pools, blending with cries of fantas
shaggy fronds weave a canopy overhead; flower blossoms the
size of cabbage heads scent the air with jasmine, a bull elephant
trumpets in the distance; and she is as primitive as her mirage,
a savage woman, bounding through the brush in a place where
mates are nonexistent, children are the product of instinct,
where anxiety is released in howls.

ARBORVITAE TREES surround Grace's backyard, so she
feels fairly confident that she cannot be seen crawling off the
porch into the overgrown grass, hoping to sustain the preter-
natural high of her shower mirage. As she ambles through the
grass, she finds it welcoming, soft and pungent with sun. The
peony blossoms are larger than her fist, and she buries her nose
in a fuchsia bloom. Goldfinches and sparrows twitter from
perches high among the leaves. *Why not try a howl or two?*

Grace tilts her chin upward and releases an experimental
howl, which sounds feeble and dovelike. She is about to give it
another go when something springs from beneath the crawl
space under her porch.

The dog is crouched low in a stalking position, and it takes
two slow steps forward, eyeing the yard, until it spots Grace.
She is not frightened; the dog couldn't weigh fifteen pounds.
His ribs are too prominent. It is perhaps the ugliest dog she has
seen. His coat is grayish-brown, matted and snarled, his eyes
are hollow and wet, and one ear is half missing. As Grace lowers into a sitting position, the dog straightens up and bares his
snaggle-toothed mouth. Grace knows from experience with

Buddy that this is not a threat; his ears are raised, not his hackles. It is a fear response, and she remains as still as possible. She also reforms her opinion—this *is* the ugliest dog she has seen.

Moments pass as the pair stare at each other. Grace is aware of dozens of dandelions between them; bright polka dots of light. She checks for a collar and tags, and seeing no glint of metal, considers calling Animal Control. Who would adopt this dog? How long before he was put down? Befriending the dog is out of the question; he's wild and may be diseased. She would need to take him to a vet, and before that, he would need grooming or at least a bath. Grace imagines his fur beneath her hand would feel like a week-old SOS pad. She will simply turn her head away and the dog will run.

When she turns back to face the house, she sees the dog's shaggy tail sliding under the porch.

ON THE ONE hand, Grace can find no practical reason to give up her new mode of ambulating. During the weeks since she became quadrupedal, she has been pain-free, her sinuses have cleared, and her pale complexion has turned rosy. Being low to the ground has enlivened her senses; she enjoys the scents of moss and warm hardwood floors, she has seen ladybugs climbing grass blades, and the increased circulation in her arms has made her hands more sensitive to touch. These are bonuses.

Before she began walking on all fours, Grace would wake each morning expecting something to happen: a telephone call, a letter, a knock on the door. She had briefly considering looking for a job, but that would have meant leaving the house, the possibility of missing something. Besides, she didn't need a job. The mortgage was paid, she had health insurance, and Roger mailed a check each month in envelopes bearing stamps of fur seals, moose grazing, totem poles, or salmon jumping from icy waters. Grace had felt frozen.

The greatest benefit of her change has been the thaw: dissipation of a sense of suspension that has gripped her for the past year, and now she doesn't miss a thing.

On the other hand, there are some things she can't do on all fours, although she has managed to narrow them down considerably. Grocery shopping is the worst and requires the greatest amount of time in an upright position. First, she has to drive, and the vast amount of space spread against the windshield makes her head dizzy and her hands sweat against the steering wheel. The carts aren't so bad; she can cross her arms on the handle and push with her elbows, allowing her body to slump enough for comfort. When her children were young, Grace would spend a full hour at Mike's Market. Now she speeds through the aisles she has streamlined her life into: fresh produce, bakery, dairy, and household.

She has removed all foodstuffs from her overhead cupboards and lowered refrigerated items to the bottom-most shelf. She's altered her diet to accommodate her four-leggedness, and in so doing, eliminated the need to stand at the sink washing dishes and stand at the stove tending pots. Rather than sitting in the kitchen opposite an empty chair, Grace eats outside on the porch.

Cupped in her newly sensitive hands, avocados feel sleek and taut as eel skin; celery stalks are like clamshells, ridged on one side, scooped and smooth on the other; peanuts offer a textural delight—dozens of miniature squares on the shells, the dry snap under her thumb, the twin toes nestled inside sienna skin so fragile that she removes it by rolling the nuts between her palms.

And, during these passing weeks, Grace has frequently shared her food with Roger—the name she's given the mangy mutt that seems to have taken up temporary residence beneath her porch. This name was not bestowed with kindness; Grace feels pleasure in throwing the corner of a sandwich, a bit of whatever she is eating, on the ground and saying, "Enjoy, Roger, you dirty dog."

Roger has not yet come within more than five feet of Grace, and she has not once reached her hand toward the dog. At first he would leap under the porch whenever Grace opened the back door. Then he began following at a distance during her afternoon crawl around the backyard.

City trucks pick up trash on Lantern Hill Lane every Tuesday morning at 7:00. Grace used to drag a twenty-gallon aluminum trash can to the curbside on Monday nights. Since her conversion, she has little disposable material and need only set the trash out once a month at 6:00 in the morning in a plastic bag clenched between her teeth. Last Tuesday, Roger slunk along behind Grace, eyes darting, nose twitching for danger. She did not find this endearing. She is certain the dog will soon leave.

THE DOG has not left by September 21, Grace's fiftieth birthday. He has taken to venturing out from under the porch when she is not outside, urinating on her arborvitae trees, pooping in what was once her petunia bed. He's in the yard now, chewing on the bark of her maple tree. As Grace watches him through the window, she wonders about his age and guesses anywhere from two to six years. She wonders where he was born, how far and long he traveled to get here, and how he must have been mistreated along the way. Grace recalls the time, years ago, when Buddy chewed the tassels off a pair of her husband's Johnson & Murphy loafers. Roger kicked Buddy, hard enough to make him howl, making Grace deeply ashamed of her husband's lack of control. Buddy had avoided him for a few hours afterward, but when Roger took Buddy's leash from the shelf, Buddy spun around, wagging his tail, and licked Roger's hand.

Roger the dog is now stretched out in the grass, rolling around with his tongue lolling out between his crooked teeth.

"Dogs don't hold grudges," Grace says. She is suddenly aware that Roger is the perfect realization of the concept "live for today." He does not fret over the past or worry about the future; he just moves forward with his nose to the ground.

Grace hears the mail drop between the front and screen doors, counts to ten, giving the postman time to move to the next house, then crawls to the door. Although her children are scattered throughout the country, they phone on occasion, and they never forget her birthday.

However, she can't hold onto the bundle of mail and move to the couch on all fours. She stands and hurries to the couch, eager to unwrap the surprises wrapped in brown paper.

The first package she opens is from her son Jason, an engineer living in Sausalito. Inside is a silver picture frame containing a photo of Jason and Patra standing in front of a Queen Anne–style house. The birthday card is signed:

Our first home. Hope you can visit us soon.
Love,

Jason and Patra

Grace takes in every detail of the stately old home, the large bay window, the lacy ornamental spindles, the stained glass of the turret window. She runs a finger over the smiling faces of her son and daughter-in-law.

Reed, her son who lives in Phoenix, sent a cassette tape. She recognizes his block lettering on the label: HAPPY BIRTH-DAY, MOM—A BONELESS ICE CREAM'S PRODUCTION. Grace walks down the hall to the linen closet, thinking only of the cassette player inside. She returns to the couch, sets the tape into the machine, and pushes Play.

Happy Birthday, Mom
Happy Birthday, Mom
You're cool, you rock, you're bomb
Don't go thinking you're over the hill
Have some cake and beer and chill
Happy Birthday, Mom
Happy Birthday, Mom
You're cool, you rock, you're bomb.

Laughing, Grace hits the Rewind button. Reed has an MFA and teaches music at the Indian School Road elementary school. He has told Grace that his band, the Boneless Ice Creams, plays weekends at local bars. She replays the tape three times before reaching for the last package.

Kristine, a student at the Chicago Art Institute School, has sent a bag of jelly beans and a poster reproduction of a Diane Arbus photograph: a transvestite sitting on a park bench with his mother. She had written across the bottom of the poster:

Happy Birthday, Mommy

Intellectually, Grace tells herself, *You have been a good mother, instilled in them enough confidence to leave home and make new lives where their hopes led them.* Emotionally, she would give anything to turn back time just for one day to ten years ago, when the house was resonant with their voices, redolent with their bodies, and for this one day she wouldn't take a moment for granted.

Grace rubs the tears from her eyes. "God, I'm so proud of them," she shouts. And an urge overcomes her to share this pride; does Roger know about the lives of his brilliant and precious children?

She quickly opens the two remaining envelopes. One is a card from her parents, and the other is a card from her sister in Kalamazoo, but nothing from Roger. Even though he had never sent anything but a check in his envelopes, and when they were together he depended on the children to remind him of Grace's birthday, this irks her more than she knew it should. A birthday card is an easy, noncommittal gesture of regard, and she deserves that much, at least.

Grace picks up the cassette player and the bag of jelly beans.

She walks out the back door and sits on the grass, placing the machine beside her. She can smell autumn riding on a breeze from the north. The leaves on her maple tree are crimson, green and gold, tangerine, and the sky is so brilliantly blue, the leaves stand out as if seen through the View Master she had as a child.

She pops a lemon jelly bean into her mouth, and Roger scrambles out from under the porch. Grace tosses him a jelly bean and hits the Play button. Roger chews vigorously, turning his head sideways with the effort, appearing to Grace to be lip-synching, "Happy Birthday, Mom."

THIS OCTOBER morning finds Grace in bed, again reading the letter from Roger she received yesterday.

Dear Grace,

I finally have the courage to tell you
I won't be coming back. Living in Alaska has
   changed me.
I wish I could have been a better husband.
I met someone here and we're expecting a baby in April.
Go ahead and file for divorce if you like.
Marriage is not important to Rain and me.
I'll keep sending money until you tell me otherwise.

                                    Roger Van Houghton

Grace rips the note in half, in quarters, in eighths, until the pieces are too small to tear and she flings them into the air. She rolls out of bed, pulls on a sweatsuit, and crawls to the top of the stairs. Through the high window of her front door, she sees a red Saturn pulling into the driveway of the house catty-corner from her own. She recognizes the car belonging to Cora Ladinsky, the girl with all the orchids in her window. A man is driving, and on the side of the car are large painted letters, half washed away, but Grace can fill in the gaps: JUST MARRIED. She watches them as they walk to the house, his arm draped casually around her hips.

Grace backward crawls down the steps, and on the way she hears a sound she's not heard in months, one she had nearly forgotten—dog's nails scratching on the door. She crawls to the kitchen and takes a loaf of nine-grain bread from the cupboard, then out the door to find Roger sitting only a foot from the porch. She sits on the stoop and tears the loaf in half, in quarters, in eighths, then flings them across the yard.

Roger eagerly moves from chunk to chunk, and Grace notices that his ribs no longer show and his coat seems cleaner. She admires the practical design of his body, how evenly distributed his weight is on his four feet, how effortlessly his path of motion responds to the scent of food. She then wonders what had motivated the first primates to push their hands against a tree, grasp hold of a low branch, and pull their spines upward. What would they need that they couldn't find close to the ground? What force would be great enough to compel them to stand, to see farther, and to move faster?

Grace considers this question a long while, until her concentration is broken by a weight in her lap, and gently she places her hand on top of Roger's head.

GRACE SITS on the grass, her lap full of bulbs. It did not take long to dig them up, much easier on all fours than squatting, thigh muscles cramping. Her fingernails are packed black and dirt breaks away from her fingers as she slides them between the seams of the parent bulbs and the new bulbettes. Grace does not hurry through this satisfying task. Roger watches her with keen interest; he had been the impetus for Grace to revive this autumn ritual, after he dug up one of Buddy's long-buried soup bones. Grace had thought, *Yes, if something you want lies buried, dig until you find it.*

She divides the bulbs in two piles, the mature bulbs and the young bulbs, and wonders why it took so long for her to embrace her own separateness.

The setting sun casts coral pink light on the bulbs. Grace believes she sees them shrug, and she leans over for closer study. Roger moves near to her side and lowers his head to sniff the bulbs. He licks her jaw and sniffs again. She knows this is a submissive gesture intended to urge food sharing, but appreciates it nonetheless.

She thinks about placing the bulbs back into the ground, points up on the soft bottom, and how they will rest through winter immersed in silence, surrounded by fragrant blackness, absolutely still, potential curled in on itself. Nobody will tell them to straighten up; they will know when the time is right, they will feel it and be unable to resist.

Sloth

The Second Sin
Sloth

H A R R I E T   H A S become a crow. She is standing in the doorway of my den dressed in a black sweatsuit, her feet turned outward in yellow tennis shoes, the hands on hips making wings of her arms. Her black hair is twisted tightly into a bun, her head thrust forward. She opens her mouth and caws, "Cal! Cal, are you listening to me?"

I venture a glance toward the door, but she is too frightening. Her dark eyes seem to be sizing up a worm. "All right, Calvin Blanchard, I'm going to stand here until you get out of that nasty old chair and come walking with me."

"Okey-dokey," I say. I will ignore the old crow, my wife of forty-six years. I will continue watching this fascinating program on body-painting practices of the Wodaabe tribe of Niger.

Harriet takes two steps into the room and surveys my haven with an expression only a recently retired first-grade teacher can muster. "Pigs live in sties, people live in homes," she says. "You disappoint me, Cal."

I am a pig, a worm, and a disappointment. I am seventy years old, short, bald, and skinny. My nickname as a kid was

Popeye, obviously in reference to my eyes and not my strength. I worked over half my life as a tailor, and since retiring two years ago, I have found my greatest peace in this room. Wrappings from cheese slices and hard candy, two years' worth of mail, *TV Guide,* newspapers, and back issues of *Reader's Digest* have accumulated underfoot. The coffee table is stacked with empty sardine tins and plastic microwave containers with forks stuck in the dried remains.

Harriet flaps her wings and says, "It's like a sauna in here." She hops to the thermostat and turns it down, then switches off my humidifier. We haven't slept in the same bed since her "change," when she drove me out by keeping the windows open and only one blanket on the bed. My arthritis can't take that.

The Wodaabe men are painting white lines down their noses, white dots on cheeks, chins, and foreheads, blackening their lips and eyes with ground charcoal. They are preparing for the *geerewol,* a male beauty contest in which they strut, painted and dressed in elaborate costumes, before the Wodaabe women. I should move to Niger; I would not be noticed. I would blend in with the dirt.

I sleep in this room, eat in this room, read in this room, and I watch TV in this room; the large, east-facing window directs sunlight on my easy chair, and I bask for hours in complete happiness.

Harriet shoves a pile of laundry off the couch and perches on the edge of the cushions. Her insistence that I get out of the house for my own good confuses me. My "good" was not a concern of Harriet's while she was teaching. Wrapped up in a world of lesson plans, evaluations, conferences, and school events, she left me on my own to settle into retirement. I took to it like a duck to water, and now, for reasons known only to her, she is making waves.

"For the life of me, I can't understand how a man who made handsome clothes for a living cares so little about his appearance."

Why does she refer to me in the third person? And why isn't it obvious that because I *had* to wear and make suits for years, I should be able to wear whatever I like, pajamas at noon, old khakis and flannel shirts, even my birthday suit should the mood strike. She pecks through the laundry and holds out a green cardigan. I relent; an hour at the blasted mall walking next to Harriet earns hours of undisturbed contentment later.

"CAL! DO you have lead in your pants? Take your hands out of your pockets and pick up your pace."

"Okey-dokey," I say, and watch Harriet charge toward the JC Penney wing. I drift to the left, where a jungle of craft booths provides adequate camouflage for the moment when Harriet discovers my defection. I wander past ceramic jack-o'-lanterns and papier-mâché turkeys, hoping to happen upon a bench. I do not like shopping malls, the fluorescent ceiling lights, the recycled air, the "retirement walkers." And there—right there—is a chain tailor shop that is most certainly staffed with morons who couldn't sew a perfect seam to save their sorry lives, but that's not my worry.

I see an empty bench next to a kiosk where a robust young

woman is cramming carrots into a machine that buzzes like a chain saw. I slide onto the bench unnoticed and watch her feed an apple into the grinder. A golden orange liquid streams from the lip of the machine into a glass pitcher. Orange is my favorite color, although no one knows this fact. It's not really a secret I've kept, because no one has ever cared to ask me my favorite color, which I would not have offered at any rate.

The woman looks about expectantly for customers, and I turn my gaze to a toy store window. If I had grandchildren, I might actually look at the stuff inside the window rather than gazing through it, but since we have no children, it's a moot point.

"Pardon me, sir. Would you like to sample some delicious and healthy juice made fresh a moment ago?"

Dang, if she isn't standing right next to me, a plastic cup held out like she's offering me the Holy Grail filled with ambrosia. Acceptance is the path of least resistance; I drink the juice. This could be the most delicious liquid ever to cross my palate: sweet, slightly nutty, tangy.

Now the woman launches into her sales spiel. When she stops for a breath, I hold up my hand, palm out. I take my credit card from my wallet and hand it to her.

She is bagging the juicer when an intercom voice announces: "Calvin Blanchard, please meet your wife at the Information Desk."

"That's you," the woman says, her enthusiasm with a sale making her gush. "I just know your wife will love it."

I bob my head and begin making my way to the Information Desk, wondering if my purchase will forfeit the promise of peace that I thought I'd earned.

"CAL! CAL, you left that bin full of carrot pulp again. Remember the agreement we made, Calvin?" Harriet's coming toward my den, her voice preceding her like the trumpets of Gideon. She had been unhappy at first with the cost of the juicer. "You're not John D. Rockefeller. You know we have to live on Social Security from now on."

Harriet handles the finances since my retirement. I've seen a bank statement or two, and I know she has a tidy nest egg stashed away, but I feel no desire to be directly involved anymore. The juicer might have caused me more problems than it was worth. However, since I now go to City Market once a week to buy carrots, she hasn't mentioned the price because we have a "weekly outing."

Harriet pokes her head through the door and I know I must turn around, away from the window from which I've been admiring a ghostly ring around the moon.

"Your machine—your mess—your cleanup."

She's dressed for bed in gray pajamas and a black robe appliquéd with white sheep. Harriet's always been stocky, but I believe her neck is disappearing into her shoulders.

"This is the fifth time in the past two weeks that you've left it overnight, and I don't appreciate the scent of fermenting carrot pulp when I come down for breakfast. A person who keeps his word is a person who can be trusted. A person who breaks his word is a person who cannot be trusted."

Harriet talks to me as if I were one of her first-grade students. Why can't she adjust, why can't she sit still and be quiet?

I wouldn't mind if she came in here and spent an hour with me before bedtime, if she could just be quiet.

"I work hard to keep this house clean while you sit in here taking root. I agreed to leave this sty alone—and I have kept my word, Calvin—but I expect you to keep yours. And after you empty the bin, don't forget to put out the trash."

"Okey-dokey. 'Night, Harriet," I say, and turn back to the window. I hear her feet, step, step, step closer, I smell the Porcelana cream on her face as she bends to peck my cheek. I think her nose is sharpening too.

MY INTERNAL clock regulates my sleeping hours. It's natural to nap after a meal, which is why I nap for an hour after breakfast, lunch, and dinner. I watch television from 9:00 P.M. to midnight, sleep until 5:00 A.M., then get a doughnut and milk from the kitchen. Harriet does not rise until 6:30, lucky for me because I forgot to empty the pulp and take out the trash last night.

Dang, it's cold outside, cold enough to see my breath. Is there any other circumstance in which you can see something that is normally invisible to the human eye? I know it's not truly my breath I'm seeing, it's . . . Grace Van Houghton from next door. She's heading for the curb on all fours with a plastic bag between her teeth and a dog trotting beside her. Harriet says Grace went around the bend after her husband left, but I don't believe that's true.

Back inside my sanctuary, I remove all my clothes, allowing the radiator's warmth and the humidifier's moisture to soak into my body. It's marvelous, and I sink sleepy-headed into my chair.

"Cal? Calvin Blanchard, where are you?"

I open my eyes to find Harriet standing three feet away.

"Harriet," I say, and she hops from one foot to the other.

"You scared the life out of me!" she shrieks.

Obviously an untruth, she's still erect. She slips her glasses down from atop her head and peers at me.

"Cal, your skin is orange. Without my glasses on, you blend right into your nasty old chair. Put some clothes on, for goodness sake." Harriet rolls her eyes upward and I see a red spot on the white below her irises. "You've been drinking too much carrot juice. You are going to return that machine. Where is the receipt?"

"In the box, I guess, over there." I point to a corner; Harriet snatches up the box and huffs out of the room. I examine my arms, which do indeed seem to match the chair in hue. Why had I not noticed this change? Is it possible the carrots are not entirely responsible? Might I, like the snowshoe hare, be blending into my environment as a survival mechanism?

HARRIET, UNABLE to find the juicer receipt in its box, is flapping around my den, her feathers ruffled. I slip out through the kitchen into the backyard. The weather is unseasonably warm for October. The leaves swish around my ankles, and I see that Harriet has propped a rake against the white oak as a reminder. I decide it's best to rake once, after all the leaves have fallen, and I sit with my back against the tree.

A squirrel leaps close to me, her mouth full of leaves, and with a bound, scurries up the tree. I tip my head back and watch her climb to a high branch where she stuffs the leaves into a nest in progress. She descends, unnerved by my presence, and hops into the Delaneys' yard. She's returning with another bunch of leaves when a rock sails through the air and smacks against her head. The squirrel falls onto her side.

Jake Delaney approaches, slouching, shifting his eyes about, a slingshot held in his right hand. I think he's eight years old, but he could be younger and just big for his age; Ed Delaney is six-four. I don't want to talk to the boy; I don't have anything to say. It's good fortune that Harriet's engaged in receipt hunting. If she had been watching from the window, the boy would get a ten-minute lecture before she marched him home and started in on Ed and Megan.

Jake slouches over the squirrel. He's so close I could count the freckles on his nose. He nudges the squirrel with his foot, she leaps onto the oak and is gone in a tail-waving flurry. Jake jumps backward, the slingshot drops, and his gaze follows the squirrel halfway up the tree. As he looks down, I remain quiet, preparing myself for Jake's startled reaction and what I might say in explanation. But his pale blue eyes pass right over me as if I had disappeared into the bark. He picks up his slingshot and runs bawling from my backyard.

~

"CAL! CALVIN, come here this instant!"

I'm in the kitchen, where I have just bitten into a sardine-topped cracker. Before I can swallow, Harriet's beside me. She's puffed up with irritation and she points a finger at the window. "That's a disgusting sight. I want you to get the shovel and bury that poor animal."

I look out the window and see crows—"a murder," I believe, is the correct term for a group of crows—feasting on a dead squirrel. Harriet turns to face me, her hands on her hips. "You have a lazy eye. Your left eye drifts when you chew. You should see a doctor."

"It's always drifted," I say. I think she's jealous because my vision is 20/20.

Harriet raps her knuckles on the window and the crows rise up squawking. "Put down the food and bury that squirrel now, Calvin. And deep enough that raccoons or possums won't dig it up." Her fist hangs in midair, and for an instant I believe she may strike me.

"Okey-dokey," I say, and head for the door leading into the garage.

"Don't dawdle, Calvin. I expect to leave for City Market at ten."

I slide the shovel under the squirrel and carry it to the arborvitae hedge separating our yard from Grace Van Houghton's. Knowing this corner cannot be seen from the house, I deposit the body beneath the hedge, then rest on the shovel handle and watch the crows land in Grace's white birch.

I HAVE paid for three dozen carrots and I'm considering going to the market's west building for a sweet roll when I hear Harriet's voice. She is not cawing, but saying "Perry Haines" as if she had a mouth full of honey. I look over my shoulder and see that she's talking to a young man. With Harriet thus engaged, I'm confident I can slip past her into the corridor connecting the two buildings. Just as I'm about to pass them, Perry hugs Harriet. Her profile softens and a smile crosses her lips, lifting her face into something lighter.

"Mrs. Blanchard, if you had not straightened me out in first grade, I probably would have ended up in reform school," Perry says. He's tall and well-groomed, wearing a cashmere blend topcoat.

"You were a bright boy, Perry. You just needed some encouragement and direction. What are you doing now?" Harriet asks.

"I'm the owner of Destiny Travel. Does Mr. Blanchard still have his shop? You know, he made the alterations on my first suit, the one I wore to job interviews."

"He's here; he was right next to me a moment ago," Harriet says, and cranes her neck about. Perry is scanning the crowd too. They both look right through me. I don't remember him. I might remember his suit, but I have no interest in getting pulled into this stroll down memory lane. I am Bacchus, God of the harvest, blending into the bounty of City Market, strolling toward the booth of plentiful sweets.

All the way home in the car Harriet chatters about Perry Haines, how kind it was of him to stop and greet her, how he assured her that should we decide to take a trip, he would find us the best accommodations at the most economical price. "When was the last time we took a vacation, Cal?"

I shrug.

"I can tell you when," Harriet snaps. If she already knew,

why bother asking? "Seven years ago we drove to Toronto and spent four days there. Don't you think it's time we had a true vacation, Calvin?"

She says this as if she has asked repeatedly over the past seven years and I've refused, which is definitely not the case.

"I'm going to Perry's establishment tomorrow afternoon and pick up some brochures."

"Okey-dokey," I say.

IT IS MY fervent hope that Harriet has a good, long yak at the travel agency with her former student. The AMC channel is showing *Charlie Chan in Paris,* and I'd like to watch it in peace. I'll just nip into the kitchen for the can of mixed nuts. What's that boy doing with a ladder? From the window, I see Jake Delaney lugging a ladder through his yard. He's wearing a mask and a cape, even though Halloween is two weeks passed. He leans the ladder against a huge maple and I watch him climb toward a tree house.

Uh-oh, the ladder is slipping off the bark, and I bang on the window hard. Jake turns his head, and I put both my hands up to indicate that he should hold still. But he doesn't see me; fear has made me transparent as the glass. Now a figure runs into my line of vision, moving in short, choppy steps. Arnold Timmick must have been on his way back to work after lunch. He reaches the ladder and steadies the base while Jake climbs down. I see him point at the boy's mask, a bright yellow alien thing that covers his whole face. Arnie repositions the ladder and holds on with both hands, but the boy, who is only about an inch shorter than Arnie, shakes his masked head. Arnie says a few more words then walks away.

Somebody ought to keep a better eye on that kid. However, this is not my worry, I have an appointment with detective Chan. I take the can of nuts from the cupboard, and dang, the kid is headed up the ladder again.

I go out the kitchen door and cross the yard. Jake sees me coming and he climbs down and sits on the ground. I don't know how to talk to children, whether or not you're supposed to make a joke, which I can't do to save my soul. I figure he already received a lecture on safety from Arnold Timmick, so I hold out the can of nuts. Jake takes a handful, and I say, "Nice tree house."

He pokes a pecan through the mask's mouth hole. "My dad built it. He's sick. He's been in the hospital a long time. He used to lift me up there on his shoulders. Mr. Timmick says I shouldn't climb a ladder unless someone holds the base."

I help myself to a walnut and look up at the tree house.

"I like being up there in the summer," Jake says. "Nobody can see me. Now with all the leaves gone people can look in the window. I want to cover it with my cape."

"Jake—Jacob Delaney," Megan calls from her back porch. Her voice sounds tired and exasperated, like Harriet's most of the time. The boy gets to his feet and slouches toward his house.

HARRIET'S KEYS jingle in the lock as Charlie Chan is about to reveal the killer in the sewers beneath Paris. *Please*

don't come in here, please let me blend into the furniture, please give me ten minutes more of—

"Calvin, I want you to look through these brochures."

Harriet drops onto the couch; she hasn't removed her jacket, nor has she looked up from the armload of glossy pamphlets she carries. I keep watching as Charlie Chan strokes his mustache thoughtfully.

Click, the set goes dark, Harriet has picked up the remote without my noticing. She's standing over me, immense in her anger, the brochures clutched and held like a torch.

"Calvin, I need a change of scenery and I'm sick of being in this house. I'm sick of seeing you in that chair all the time. Don't you want to see the world beyond this room? Don't you want to meet people and make friends?"

My brain protests, thinking through the awful possibilities of traveling with Harriet. I would like to tell her that I don't want people around me, that I lose bits of myself each time I come in contact with another person. Only when I am alone am I truly free. "I'm happy here," I say.

"I'm not happy, Cal. Look at this cruise brochure for seniors. See the couple dancing on the deck under the stars? I want to dance under the stars. You never touch me anymore, Calvin. When did you stop touching me?"

I would be an idiot as well as a worm to speak the truth and say it was when she drove me out of our bed.

Now Harriet's shoulders sag and her body seems to deflate. This would be the moment I should stand and put my arms around her. Instead I think of the hundreds of bodies I fitted for suits and shirts, the constant awareness of them, the closeness, the tape against the shoulders, the arms, waist, along the thigh and down to the ankles, me on my knees, cautious not to linger with a measurement, silent and anonymous.

"I give up!" Harriet caws, startling me. I cast a sideways glance and see her throw the brochures into the air, watch them flutter to the floor like a flock of tropical birds.

IT'S 11:00 P.M., and not wishing to view the latest victims of whatever crime is being featured on the news, I mute the set and look for a magazine. The first thing to catch my eye is the dancing couple on the deck, the single brochure that landed on my coffee table. They look like the couple in those Ensure ads. How is it that an intelligent woman like Harriet can be suckered into this illusion? They're professional models making a pretty penny for the bodies they sweat to keep firm and their ability to masquerade romance.

I climb the stairs and enter Harriet's bedroom. Isn't it curious how moonlight can travel through a black sky, enter a window and change everything? She's lying on her side, right arm under the pillow, left arm extended, legs drawn up slightly into the curve where I used to sleep soundly. I walk close to the bed. With her black hair spread over the pillow, her lashes long in sleep, her mouth sweet in repose, Harriet is as pretty as Snow White, and I bend and gently kiss her cheek.

The curtains flap with a cold wind, and I lower the pane an inch. I look out and see Jake's tree house; from this viewpoint, I can see through the window, see a small table and crayon drawings tacked to the wall. Rectangular pieces of wood have been nailed to the tree at twelve-inch intervals from trunk to tree house, Arnie's doing, I'd guess. The light hue of the new wooden rungs stand out in the moonlight, and I'm overtaken with a sudden urge to be looking at this window from inside Jake's tree house.

I descend the stairs, round the corner, and go down the basement stairs. I remove the sheet from my Singer, then run my finger along fabric stacked beside the machine. I find two yards of midnight-blue bunting left over from miniature Michigan flags I'd made for Harriet's class in '76. I open the drawer, find the blue-wrapped bobbin, thread the needle, and begin.

HAVE I ever been outside at 3:00 in the morning? Perhaps on a still, hot summer night of my youth, certainly not in November. Only the wind and I move through Lantern Hill Lane. Shadows of trees rake long fingers over the lawns, and my own moon shadow stretches out long and tall. Me and my shadow, climbing the tree house stairs, holding blue curtains and a pressure rod.

I have them up in a moment, the left panel bearing a radiant sun, sort of Aztec in design, and the right bearing a crescent moon with a star hanging from a moonbeam on the bottom arc. Now, I part the curtains and look across at the window where I stood four hours ago, expecting to meet a ghost of myself staring back. Only glass, not even a reflection of trees or moon. Clouds have blown in, full, black-bottomed clouds, white-topped like huge ships moving through a dark sea. I'm on the verge of remembering something, but it passes and I descend on the wooden blocks.

The wind has died, replaced by stillness so inviting that I close my eyes and hold my breath. And the clouds open, as if their seams have broken under pressure, releasing flurries of snow. Before I reach my backyard, the ground is white, my jacket is white, and my bald head is capped white. I turn around to find I have left no footprints. I walk toward the house, becoming lighter with each step, and beneath Harriet's window my body disintegrates among the swirling snow and I dance and dance.

Wednesday

Wednesday's Child
Is Full of Woe

$\mathcal{E}$D DELANEY removes his gloves and lights the hand warmer. The kerosene heater would have been warmer, but then the deer might smell it, and this is his last chance. The sun will be up in about twenty minutes. He pushes an orange crate through the few inches of snow, rubbing it into the semi-frozen ground. His mother-in-law had been right about the deer. She'd called him at the hospital and said she and her friend were sitting in the car in her driveway talking when they saw a deer come down the hill. She said it ate crab apples on the ground, and wasn't it funny that all the men had gone up north to hunt, and there was a deer right in her own back-yard. Ed saw the tracks this morning when he came up the hill and got down close to the ground around the tree.

He puts the red plastic hot seat on the crate and settles in, Styrofoam squishing under his weight. There is some light now coming through the naked treetops, enough to see a cardinal in the bush a few yards away. He knows it's a male; his red is brilliant against the snow.

Ed pulls his stocking hat farther down over his earmuffs.

His head gets so cold outdoors. Dave Walters had used an ice cap when he had chemo, and it saved his hair. But Ed knows it doesn't really matter; it's all a matter of time anyway.

He raises his Winchester 32 Special to his shoulder, sighting, then lowers it across his knees and runs his hand down the custom-made mahogany stock. This is a fine gun. This gun has brought down four bucks. He remembers each one well.

The sun is beginning to swell pale yellows. He notices the breeze is slight, just teasing the few clinging, shaky leaves. Ed's position is good; he is downwind from the crest of the hill.

His wife gave him some hell for coming out, but not too much. He wishes she would have given him a lot more just so he could say, "Megan, don't get your Irish up," and hope she would go off on an angry tirade like she used to do. He thinks about her smile, how, following those first desperate days after the diagnosis, her smile became too easy, artificial. And he smiled back at her then, in the weeks of denial and hope. Then he stopped—but Megan kept smiling through his angry raging weeks, his silent, withdrawn, bargaining-with-God weeks, his weeping, suicidal weeks, until finally acceptance came sweet and calming as an injection of morphine. He knows that as an emergency room nurse, Megan is accustomed to quick resolution; you save a life in minutes, or you lose one in hours. Losing him to the slow, ugly progression of this disease is unacceptable, unthinkable for her. He wishes he could talk with her about the changes she needs to make, but he loves her too much to get past that smile.

He begins to shudder, then thinks of the words to a song. This technique works, a practiced technique, mind over matter; he gets cold quickly, so easily now. It's good to be outside, far away from transfusions and needles and uncomfortable friends with empty faces shifting in bedside chairs.

It's quiet too, except for some traffic noise from the highway down in front of the house. This is a hell of a place to hunt, but Ed wants to taste venison this year. Not someone else's venison—his, from the deer *he* brings down. When his father-in-law called yesterday, he said Bob had got an eight-point, but none of the other guys had any luck. They were all up there, at the camp near Traverse City. That's where he'd gotten his four. He hopes they'll call tonight. After they eat dinner, they'll all go into town and drink beer and retell hunting stories of today and the seasons before. He'll tell them tonight about the buck, twelve or fourteen points, how it was bending its neck to eat crab apples when he fired the shot.

The sun's up now. The birds are calling. They'll settle in the crab apples to feed, and he'll watch for them all to rise at once in a wave when the buck comes. Ed releases the safety and gets set, still. What is that calling, a mourning dove? No, it's an owl, an owl on the hunt for rabbits or field mice. It's closer now. That story from Boy Scouts, Indian folklore. The owl has called my name.

He'll tell Jake tonight that when he was out hunting, he heard an owl and it called out his name, and when he's old enough to be a Scout, he'll hear that story about the Indian who heard the owl call his name, and then he'll remember the night his dad brought home a buck and promised him the antlers and told him the story about the owl calling his dad's name, before he went back to the hospital, and he hopes Jake doesn't cry, and he can't cry now; the buck is approaching.

Anger

The Third Sin

Anger

$\mathcal{T}$HE E.R. charge nurse assesses the man's injuries and directs the EMT to Exam Room 5. Megan Delaney exits Room 4 and follows the gurney, her quick steps squeaking on the tile floor. The EMT tells the man to get up onto the exam table. He tells Megan the man's vitals are normal and leaves the room.

The patient is in his twenties, buzz-cut orange hair, dressed in jeans, white T-shirt, leather jacket, and motorcycle boots. Megan does not notice his appearance; her gaze is fixed on the bloody towels wrapped around his wrists.

"You just gonna stand there gawking at me, or what?" the man snaps.

Megan carefully removes the towels. His wounds are horizontal and already clotted closed. A small flame sparks in Megan's stomach. She imagines how her husband's body must have looked after the organ donor docs were through. Ed had signed away everything except his bone marrow, which, even after a transplant, couldn't stop the multiplying leukemia cells.

"Do something, will you, Blondie? Can't you see I'm in pain?" he moans.

Blondie? Did he just call me Blondie? Megan's thought is secondary, floating somewhere above the distinct physical change occurring in her body. What began as a small flame is now a fire racing through her limbs and crackling in her ears. She steps to the sink and turns on the cold water.

"Get a doctor in here," the man says. "I need something for the pain. The only thing that works for me starts with a D. Duh ... Dem ... Demerol, that's it," he says, writhing on the table.

Megan has been shut down emotionally for eight weeks; eight weeks of ignoring Ed's belongings, eight weeks of answering phone calls and mail from those who didn't know Ed had died, eight weeks of waking up and expecting to find him beside her where he should be, eight weeks of Jake's tears.

Megan has not cried. Since Ed's diagnosis, she has held her family together with strength and a smile. She knows that if she releases herself to tears, she may never be able to stop weeping. She loved her husband more than life. Megan Delaney is a house on fire, and the windows are about to shatter.

"You want to die? You sure made a half-assed attempt," she shouts. "Get in a car, run a hose from the exhaust into the window, start the engine, you'll be dead in ten minutes, guaranteed."

The man lies still, gaping at Megan in disbelief.

"Hanging works well, just make sure the rope's tied to something sturdy before you jump." Megan steps closer to the man and he shrinks back in fear. Her jaw is clenched and her green eyes are slits of rage. "We're in the business of saving lives here, not wasting time on pathetic losers like you. Today we saved a woman hit by a drunk driver, but the surgeons couldn't save her leg. And a six-year-old with a gunshot wound is in O.R. now. In the next room, there's a blind man who was mugged and beaten. He's grateful to be alive!"

"You're fuckin' crazy," the man says, and swings his legs off the bed.

Megan opens a metal drawer and removes a scalpel. "Maybe you've watched too many movies, or maybe you're just a dumb fuck who doesn't know that you have to make the cuts vertically, elbow to wrist," she says, moving closer to the man, waving the scalpel up and down.

"Hey! Help—somebody get in here—help!"

With her free hand, Megan pushes away the wet bangs clinging to her forehead. "Who was the woman that called 911? Your girlfriend or your mother? Did she plead with you, crying at the door? Did she pray? Did you even look at her when the EMTs took you out? Should I save them a lot of future grief and do this the right way?"

"Delaney—Delaney!"

Someone grabs her arm, tugs her down the hallway, and pulls her through the E.R. doors outside the hospital to the ambulance entrance.

"Holy shit, give me the scalpel, Meg."

Megan leans against the brick wall and breathes in the January night air, breath after cooling breath. The charge nurse, Wanda Avery, looks as if she has run a marathon. Her chest heaves under the white uniform and her mouth is slack. "The scalpel, Meg?"

Megan looks at the instrument as if a magician had made

it appear out of thin air. She raises her hand and loosens her grip so the scalpel lies flat on her palm.

Wanda takes the scalpel and tucks it in her pocket, handle first. "What the devil came over you?" she pants. "Nine years in E.R. and you're the only one who's never blown a gasket."

"I don't know," Megan mumbles. But she thinks Wanda's reference to the devil is the most probable explanation. She had felt possessed.

"North's sewing him up, and someone from Psych is on the way down," Wanda says. "Too bad North's on duty. Now you know he's going to put the disciplinary committee on you."

Megan wraps her arms around herself and shivers; she can't afford to lose her job. After the medical and funeral expenses that the insurance had not covered were paid, her bank account was dismally low.

"Listen, your record's spotless, and everyone here knows what you've been through this past year. They won't suspend you, probably give you a lecture on patient rights." Wanda breaks into a grin and bends at the waist, laughing. "Guess you didn't notice the wet stain spread over the guy's jeans—you made that punk piss his pants. There's only a half hour left on your shift. You go on home."

MEGAN STAYS in her car in the driveway after she has parked. Through the window, she can see her neighbor, Gloria, sleeping on the couch. She's a student at MSU and has baby-sat for Jacob since Ed died. For a moment she considers that the woman sleeping is the mother of a boy sleeping in another room, that if she keeps driving, she'll find her own house, her own life the way it used to be. She rests her head on the steering wheel, then quickly opens the car door, overcome with a need to hold onto Jake.

Megan takes a ten dollar bill from her purse and taps Gloria's shoulder. Gloria tells her what they ate for dinner and that she and Jake played video games for a while before bedtime. She slips on her coat and waves good-bye from the doorway. Even though Megan is eager for Gloria to leave, eager to go to Jake's room and lie down beside him for a while, with this gesture the thought occurs to Megan that Gloria's husband will be waiting for her in bed. Gloria will undress, turn off the light, and fall into the breathing, warm flesh of a man who loves her.

Megan's cheeks flush with resentment, her stomach burns, and she hurries to Jake's room before she loses control. Before Ed died, Jake couldn't sleep if even a slice of light fell into his room from the hallway. Tonight his bed is faintly lit by the glow of a yellow Pokémon night-light Megan's mother bought. With its arrival, she had received a roundabout lecture on her shortcomings as a mother, how Jake sleeps so well at Grandma's house because she has a night-light. She wants to rip the damn thing from the wall and stomp on it.

As she walks toward the light, a burst of cold air touches the back of Megan's neck and she whirls about. Both windows are closed and locked. Jake is sleeping with his face down in the pillow, the same way his father slept. Megan lifts the covers and lies down beside her son. He rolls over onto his back, and from his dream murmurs, "I hope . . . I hope."

Megan squeezes her eyes shut to hold back tears. She knows what he is hoping, and that only children can harbor impossible fairy-tale hopes; all of hers are long gone. She gets out of bed and lifts the small hand dangling from the mattress to her lips. "Good night, my prince," she whispers.

She walks down the hall into her bedroom and shuts the door. The bed looms before her, immense with emptiness. Staring at the patterns in the chenille spread, the swirl and rise of nap, Megan feels her temperature rise. She sees the punk from the E.R. sneering at her from the hospital bed, she sees Ed lapsed into a coma, his final breaths gurgling as she squeezed his hand. She smells Drakkar Noir—Ed's cologne.

Megan yanks the spread to the floor, opens the closet and snatches Ed's clothes, tossing them onto the spread until the hangers are bare. She grabs a pair of loafers and hurls them at the mound of clothes. Next, the beat-up Nikes are flung through the air. "Damn you to hell, Ed Delaney! Damn you for leaving us alone."

Megan walks to Ed's dresser. Underwear, socks, T-shirts, sweaters join the pile until perspiration beads her forehead and the four drawers are empty. Then she sighs and her body shudders. She straightens her back and meets her image reflected from the mirror mounted above the dresser: dark half-moons rim her eyes and thin red lines run through the whites, her hair sticks out haywire, and when she runs her hand through it, sparks of static snap her fingertips. She thinks she might cry, she wants to cry but tears won't come.

On the dresser top is a framed senior prom photo and a large envelope from the funeral home containing Ed's effects. In the photo, Megan and Ed are standing in front of a papier-mâché rocket ship, NOTHING'S GONNA STOP US NOW painted across the nose. She's wearing a mint-green dress and a gardenia wrist corsage. Megan looks again at her reflection, and the comparison between the girl she was and the shell she's become pulls her anger into an anthropomorphous voice that whispers, *Embrace me and be purified—give me more.*

She knocks the photo to the floor and steps on the glass. She empties the envelope onto the dresser. Ed's wedding ring spins like a quarter, the revolutions thundering in her ears. There's the medal given to him by his mother two months before he died. Megan glares at the coiled chain and bright, engraved depiction of Michael, angel protector against the devil, especially at the hour of death. She grabs the medal, preparing to throw it across the room, when it seems to burn against her palm and she drops it to the floor.

The last item is Ed's wristwatch. Megan picks it up, and the flexible metal wristband is cool in her hand. She remembers the impressions left on Ed's skin every night before he went to sleep.

To sleep . . . to sleep . . . can I sleep now? What time is it?

Megan turns the face upright and sees that the date and time read the exact moment of Ed's death. She flings the watch at the pile as if a snake had wrapped around her arm and she collapses on the bed.

MEGAN WAKES two hours later, shivering. She tries to remember how much she lowered the thermostat to save on heating bills. She tucks the covers tightly about her and curls into a ball, hoping to fall back into sleep. But she begins thinking that if Ed were alive and she wouldn't be scrambling to pay bills, she wouldn't be shivering in their bed. Anger whispers in her ear, *You deserve better—I can keep you warm.*

Megan punches her pillow and mumbles, "The first night I finally *can* sleep and—"

She stops short as her hip shifts downward with the impression of someone sitting beside her. She reasons that Jake has come in because of a nightmare, and she swallows her irritation. There is no silhouette of her son in the darkened room, and glancing down, she sees an adult-size indentation in the mattress. She quickly switches on the bedside lamp, and the indentation disappears. "Delaney, is that you? If you still love me, cut this shit out."

AT 7:00 A.M., Megan rubs her eyes, feeling weak and shaky, as if waking from a twelve-hour fever. *Was I hallucinating or was Ed here last night?*

She regards the mess produced during last night's fury and groans. *I can't do this again, and I can't let Jacob see this.* She picks up the wool plaid shirt Ed had worn hunting and buries her face in the rough material, remembering how happy he was that night, how he hugged her close with one arm and lifted Jake with the other.

A thud sounds from Jake's room and Megan jumps into action. She tosses the smashed photo on top of the clothes and shoves the lot under her bed. She changes out of her wrinkled uniform into jeans and a sweater.

Megan walks down the hall and sticks her head into Jake's room.

"Are you up?"

Jake is not in his room, but she has a good idea where he's hiding. She gets her jacket and heads out the back door.

Standing beneath the tree house, Megan yells, "Jake, I know you're in there."

The sun and moon curtains move slightly. *How did those curtains get up there?* she wonders. *Someone has come onto my property, climbed the tree, and hung those curtains up. Did anyone ask me first? Are we a charity case now?*

Megan imagines her mother's voice saying, "What wonderful neighbors you have. You should do something nice for them." And she knows that voice is correct, she knows she should be grateful, but her pain keeps her short of being whole, of remembering the good neighbor she was before Ed's death ripped her in half. Anger is easy; anger makes her strong. *I suppose the whole damn street thinks I'm incapable of taking care of my own kid.*

"Jacob Delaney, you come down from there and get yourself ready for school," Megan shouts.

Jake's head pops out of the window. "I don't want to go to school. I hate school. Everyone stares at me all the time. And your face is scary now." His voice trembles with emotion, which fuels Megan's anger.

I wish my life were so simple: get dressed, eat breakfast, get on the bus, go to school, come home six hours later and have nothing to do. I have to grocery shop, do the laundry, clean the house, pay the bills, shovel the walk, take care of Jake . . . take good care of Jake.

Megan closes her eyes and makes a conscious effort to relax the muscles in her face. "I'm sorry my face was scary, Jake, it scares me too sometimes," she says. "You know what? I hate work and everybody stares at me, but I have to go because we need money to eat and to live in this house. And you have to go to school because I can't teach you everything you need to learn."

MEGAN IS listening to Oldies 97.5 on her way to Mike's Market when the music stops in the middle of the song. After a second of dead air, Bruce Hornsby's voice sings through the car speakers: "I met a fan dancer in south side Birmingham. She was running from a fat man selling salvation in his hand."

"Jacob's Ladder," Ed's favorite song, and the song that gave Jake his name. Megan has never heard it played on the radio and is so disconcerted she doesn't see the black car speeding through a red light. Ten feet from impact, the song abruptly stops and Megan sees the car. The driver flips his middle finger at Megan as she pumps the brake on their twelve-year-old Cutlass, keeping the steering wheel steady to avoid skidding on the snowy road.

Once Megan has the car under control, she sees the black, shiny piece of Jap-scrap making a left on Cedar Street. *Get the son of a bitch,* anger hisses in her ear.

Knuckles gripped white around the wheel, Megan pulls left and steps on the gas. She's nearly on top of his bumper when he turns sharply into a 7-Eleven lot. Megan follows him, her neck scarlet and her cheek twitching. She parks beside the black car and strides toward the man who has just stepped out of his car. "You could have killed me, you son of a bitch!" she shouts.

The man whips around. He's short and stocky, about forty years old, wearing a Red Wings hat and a Carhartt jacket.

"You ran a red light and then flipped me off. Do you think because I'm a woman in a beat-up old car you can pull that shit?" Megan is so close that her breath condenses on the man's glasses.

He steps back, shrugs, and spits into the snow. "Fuck off, bitch."

His words sound to Megan like a slow-running film:

Faa ... ck ... aah ... fff ... bi ... tch.

Her right hand forms a fist, arcs upward, and her knuckles slam into the soft tissue under the man's nose. His glasses fly and blood trickles from his nostrils. A woman, who had been crossing the lot, scurries inside the store. The man swipes a finger under his nose and bends to retrieve his glasses. Anger goads Megan on, *Kick him in the ass.*

She cocks her foot, adrenaline rushing to her thigh muscles. However, as her foot begins its forward swing, a sudden weight hangs around her ankle like an invisible hand pulling in the opposite direction. Her kick is delivered at half force, enough to send the man sprawling into the five-inch concrete curb. His Red Wings hat flops to the right as he rolls onto his back. A bar of swollen flesh instantly rises on his forehead. A siren wails from the cop car speeding down Cedar Street.

"JUDGING BY your expression, I guess these classes haven't improved your disposition," Vivian Flynn mutters. She peers over the rim of her coffee cup at her daughter. "My own flesh and blood nabbed by the cops, a nurse, no less—Jesus, Mary, and Joseph."

Megan throws her coat over a chair and fills a glass with water from the tap. For the past six weeks she has wasted her one night a week off on anger management classes. She crumples her five-by-seven-inch diploma and tosses it at the wastebasket.

"I was not *nabbed*. The creep didn't press charges, couldn't stand the fact that a woman cleaned his clock."

"I don't appreciate your tone of voice. If you ask me, you already need a refresher course."

Tell the old bag to go to hell, anger whispers.

"I didn't ask for your opinion, Mother. Would you care to trade places with me? Spend eight hours on your feet in the E.R., sponging up blood, cleaning up vomit, listening to people scream in pain, then go to fucking anger management class and see how well it works for you?"

"Megan Flynn, don't get your Irish up with me," Vivian says, wagging her finger at Megan, who imagines her teeth closing over that clawlike digit, biting through to the bone of the finger that's wagged at her for thirty-one years.

"And I suppose you speak to Jacob in this way. Maybe that's why he's—"

"Don't you dare start on Jake," Megan growls. Anger embraces her, fills her arms, and she pounds the table. "You have no idea what I've been going through. You have Dad, you've always had Dad: he pays the bills, buys you presents, takes you on trips, brings you flowers, pampers and spoils you, and you don't have a cold, empty bed waiting for you at the end of the day. *You* have a good life. I want my life back."

Vivian's eyes pool with tears, but this draws no sympathy from Megan. Her mother's tears are like lighter fluid squirted onto a bonfire, and Megan turns her back to regain control.

"Meggy, you need to move on. I've been reading a book about grief and the stages a person goes through. First is denial, which you seemed to have done better than anyone I know. I never saw you shed a tear, even when they lowered that sweet soul into the ground. The second stage is anger, and you've been angry for weeks, don't think I haven't noticed."

And it feels damn good, doesn't it? I make you hot, I make you alive again, and without me, you're dead to the world. Megan swallows hard; anger has his tongue down her throat, making the effort of words nearly impossible. "What's the next stage, Mother dear," Megan asks, her voice slow and deep with sarcasm.

"Bargaining, then depression, and finally acceptance," Vivian sniffs.

"Okay, Mother, I'll make a bargain with you. If you leave right now without saying another word, I won't slap that smug, know-it-all smirk off your face."

Vivian inhales sharply with a squeak then juts her chin forward. With trembling hands she opens her purse and slides the prom photograph across the table.

"Where did you get this?" Megan snaps.

Vivian presses her lips together tightly and glares at her daughter. Megan crosses her arms and grips her ribs, anger expanding like bellows inside her chest. Vivian can clam up for days if it strikes her fancy. "I'm sorry. Will you please tell me where you got this."

"Jacob went up in his tree house as soon as you left. I called and called for him to come down to dinner, but he didn't answer. He was talking, laughing too, as if someone was in there with him. I got scared, so I went across the street to the midget's house. You know I can't go up a tree with my arthritis," Vivian whines, rubbing her right knee.

Megan grips the edge of the table; her head will explode, the top of her skull will blow off and spew brains like a volcano shoots lava, if Vivian doesn't get to the point in about five seconds.

"The midget came over right away, climbed up there, and coaxed Jacob down. After we got in the house, I saw Jake was holding that picture. He started crying and said, 'Mom doesn't even miss Daddy. She never talks about him and she hid his stuff under the bed, even his best picture.' Meggy, remember the girl in that photo? The lovely, sweet-natured girl Ed fell for? Look at your beautiful dress, the sparkle in your eyes. Ed didn't take his eyes from you even for the photographer."

Megan's pulse pounds inside her neck. She grips the table tighter and opens her mouth. As her hair-raising growl is released, Megan flips the table end over end, and in a flash she's out in the night. Running toward the maple tree, she slows her pace at the sight of a white light glowing from the tree house. There, leaning against the back of the garage, is an ax. Megan grabs the handle and climbs the tree house ladder.

By the time she ducks inside, the white glow is gone. However, the moonlight is bright enough for her to see what Jake has done. She hasn't been up here since Ed died, and the change is startling. The walls are lined with Jake's crayon drawings of Ed, dozens of them: in his suit carrying his brief-case, riding his four-wheeler at Sleeping Bear Dunes, on the beach in Pentwater, shooting pool in the basement rec room, sitting in the La-Z-Boy with Jake on his lap.

Megan begins to sweat; she feels as if she's in a sauna. She hears Vivian's voice below calling, "Megan, Megan, please come down."

Slung over Jake's small chair is Ed's wool plaid shirt, the material draping over his tackle box set beside the chair. The box is open to show a photo taped inside the lid of Ed and Jake fishing on Bass Lake, Jake holding high a stringer of bluegills. Megan wipes the sweat from her forehead with her sleeve and tugs off her sweater.

On the small table are the deer antlers Ed intended to have mounted, the plastic gold cup trophy with a WORLD'S BEST FATHER sticker that Jake gave to Ed last Father's Day, and Ed's watch marking the time of his death. She pictures Jake crawl-ing under her bed and gathering all he could, all he needed, into his arms, walking to the tree house, his little face solemn with purpose, and she raises the ax. She imagines the vibrations up her arms, the splinter and break of wood, the pungent scent of cedar.

No, the scent of Drakkar Noir and a gush of frigid air pressing hard against her back. She tries to shake it off and icy arms encircle her. Megan thrashes and the ax drops danger-ously close to her feet. "Damn it! Let me go!" she screams.

Jacob's voice cuts high and thin through the dark, his bare

feet churning through the snow. "Mom—Mommy—are you okay?" He climbs until he can just peek inside and he whispers, wide-eyed, "Your whole body is smoking, Mom."

Steam rises from Megan and envelops her in a translucent cloud. Her mouth begins to turn blue and her teeth chatter. Through the cloud, in the darkness outside the tree house, she sees Ed's face wearing the same stupid, big grin he wore in that prom photo.

"Oh, honey, why did you leave us," she cries, stepping out the door, her arms outstretched. Now she is falling through tree limbs, slowly, slowly, cradled in her husband's arms. Ed's soothing baritone sings: "She said he's tryin' to save me, but I'm doin' all right, the best that I can, just a pair of fallen angels tryin' to get through the night."

Megan drifts lightly as a feather, trembling, sobbing, past Jacob, down, down to rest on the blanket of snow, her tears turned to ice and a prayer on her lips.

Thursday's Child
Has Far to Go

*G*LORIA CASTELLANI brushes her finger over her upper lip, thinking, *God, help me find the words to get out of this without blowing everything.* "Must be powdered sugar," she says. "I just ate a doughnut."

Gloria's husband sets his gun and badge on the dresser.

"That's a crime under Michigan law, Code 401, eating doughnuts in bed."

She musters a smile for Steve's joke, but she does not want to talk. She needs to lie still and wait for the nausea to subside, for her heartbeat to slow, for the China White to kick in. She had nearly been caught. Was Steve home early or had she lost track of time studying for tomorrow's exam?

Steve switches off the light and gets into bed. He drapes an arm over Gloria and pulls her close. "I thought about you all through my shift, babe," he says, cupping her breast.

Gloria can't handle sex right now. She rolls onto her side. *Five minutes, give me five more minutes.* "I'm beat from studying. I've got an exam in the morning."

"Oh, come on," Steve murmurs in her ear. "You'll ace it as usual. Just relax and let me do all the work."

Gloria feels her nightgown hiked up and Steve's penis press against her bottom. *Do not puke; don't give yourself away, come on, come on, come on . . . ah the rush, body melting into the bed, better than ten orgasms . . .* "I love you, Steve."

⌐∽⌐

THE FOLLOWING morning Gloria confronts her image in the bathroom mirror. She wets a washcloth and scrubs her face, then opens her makeup case and removes the liquid liner. While outlining her eyes she gets the impression that something looks different. She holds up a small mirror and turns sideways to examine her profile. It seems to Gloria that her nose is slightly bigger, and she thinks of the rhyme used to taunt her as a child, "Liar, Liar, pants on fire. Your nose is longer than a telephone wire."

It was only a white lie to protect Steve. It's not as if I'm an addict sticking a needle in my arm, getting exposed to HIV or hepatitis. My use is purely recreation. No harm done.

She sets the mirror aside and admires her complexion, as white and smooth as when she was a teenager. Her dark eyes are bright and inquisitive, and her black hair shines with health. "You're still gorgeous. Don't screw up."

Gloria Castellani has been snorting heroin for six months. Only Darryl knows, and he won't talk.

⌐∽⌐

WALKING DOWN Lantern Hill Lane toward the Cedar Street bus stop, Gloria runs possible exam topics through her mind: grids, hierarchies, grouping, and phrasing. Two more semesters and she'll have a Bachelor of Arts in Graphic Design. She believes that her high grade point average coupled with instructor recommendations will get her into graduate school at Parsons. She had set her sights on Parsons School of Design as a freshman—66 Fifth Avenue, NYC. Next spring a representative from Parsons will be conducting interviews at MSU. Gloria will make a good impression. She always does because she projects confidence and communicates in a forthright manner without giving up a shred of her femininity. She dresses well in solid colors, simple jewelry—and she listens with an ear toward retaining important information and discarding fluff. These traits come naturally to Gloria after twelve years of practice and determination to hide the truth that she is never going to be the best at anything she tries.

We'll move after I graduate . . . Gloria imagines she and Steve in a studio apartment in Greenwich Village. *Finally—farewell to Lansing, farewell to my past. Cops can get jobs anywhere, certainly in New York City. What about a connection? No shortage in New York, for sure, but how would I find another Darryl?*

Gloria tells herself that it doesn't matter, that she can quit the stuff whenever she wants.

STANDING INSIDE the campus canoe livery on the Red Cedar River, Gloria frames her shot, deep green pines shading the last circles of snow under their boughs, the water churning over black boulders. Photography has been a passion since she was eleven, the age when the world began to spin around her, the age she was when her mother ran away. With a camera, Gloria discovered she could enter another space and stop time, if only for a moment.

As a child, she knew her mother was different from other moms, that she always had a glass in her hand, and sometimes her voice was too loud. She was beautiful because she had long, straight shiny hair, she wore blue jeans with flowers, butterflies, and mushrooms embroidered along the legs, and she sang to Gloria in the kitchen. A few months before she left, Gloria's father had banned his wife from Amelio's, the family's restaurant.

The kids at school would ask, "Where's your mother, Gloria, where's Donna the drunk?" then stagger around the playground.

Gloria would answer, "She's visiting my aunt in Cleveland," which was her father's story.

"Liar, liar, pants on fire, your nose is longer than a telephone wire."

Everyone except Gloria knew that Mrs. Castellani had staggered aboard a Greyhound bus with two suitcases. Of course, she soon came to realize that her mother was not simply visiting relatives. Gloria drove herself to be the smartest, prettiest, best behaved daughter, and somehow her mother would find out and come back to them.

Gloria's father grieved the loss of his wife by practically living at the restaurant, leaving Gloria in the care of her older brother, Tony Junior. Big Tony Castellani didn't get enough sleep, he gained fifty pounds, and he died of congestive heart failure when Gloria was sixteen. After the funeral, when her uncle Sal suggested someone try to find her mother, Tony Junior said not to bother, that he was twenty-one and he could take care of Gloria better than Donna the drunk.

A flash of cramping seizes Gloria's abdomen and she lowers her camera. Constipation has been a recurring problem since she started using, but easily solved with a laxative. She couldn't take one this morning because of the exam and her afternoon class. Gloria raises her camera again and tries to concentrate on the shot, but she can only think that the cramps would disappear in a moment if she did a line. She could lie down on the planks, rest her head against her arm, and bliss out watching the river flow by. Gloria's fingers reach for the glassine packet tucked inside the watch pocket of her black jeans.

"Hey, Gloria, don't you ever quit?"

Gloria turns around and aims her camera at the woman walking toward her from the opposite end of the livery. It works—Heather stops to pose, and Gloria has a moment to compose herself.

"Bitch of an exam, huh," Heather says.

"Did you think it was tough?"

"Go ahead, rub it in, smartass. God, you're pale. Are you feeling okay?" Heather asks.

No, I'm not, and I won't feel okay until I get some powder up my nose. Think fast and don't screw up. Gloria pats her belly. "It's that time of the month," she lies.

"Do you want aspirin? I've got some in my backpack."

Heather slides off her pack and digs to the bottom. She hands Gloria a small metal box. Gloria releases the catch and removes two aspirin. The upper half of her face reflects from the mirror inside the box lid. Her nose seems to fill the entire surface. She closes her right eye and turns her left eye in toward her nose.

"Gloria, what *are* you doing?" Heather asks.

Gloria pops the aspirin in her mouth and hands the box back to Heather. "Something in my eye."

"Gotta run; Art History in ten minutes. Feel better," Heather says, and bounds off toward Erickson Hall.

Reflecting sunlight from the river dances on the livery wall, and Gloria remembers it was on a spring day like this one three years ago that she met Steve. She was outside on break from waiting tables at Amelio's, camera in hand, when a police car pulled someone over in front of the restaurant. The way he walked to the car with relaxed yet deliberate steps caught Gloria's attention. When he removed his sunglasses, she zoomed in on his face. She couldn't tell what he was saying to the driver. Even as his lips moved, his expression remained impassive. After he had written the ticket and the driver pulled away, he looked at Gloria and tipped his hat, as if he had been aware of her presence from the start.

A group of six ducks quack as they glide past on the surface of the river, six expanding V's trailing behind them. They are mallards, newly arrived from the south for spring breeding. Gloria understands the call of migration, a need so wild and strong, there's no reason or logic, right or wrong. She jumps off the livery onto the riverbank and hurries downstream to get a head-on shot. When she zooms in and adjusts her focus on the mallards, she sees their dark yellow feet paddling like mad just below the surface.

"THREE POINT EIGHT. You're really slipping, babe," Steve says with a laugh.

"Screw you, it's not funny. This blows my chance to grad-uate summa cum laude, even if I get a 4.0 from here on out." Gloria wants to shred the paper and flush it down the toilet. She'll talk to her prof and ask to retake the exam; she wasn't feeling well that day, she is sure she can convince him to give her a second shot.

Steve hugs her, and she tries to relax in his arms. Her limbs feel wooden, stiff and creaking at the joints. She wants him out of the house so she can get high.

He rubs her back and says, "Spring break starts in a couple of weeks. I have a week of vacation and five sick days built up. We could drive to Florida. Sun, sand, you on the beach in that little red bikini—ow!" Steve exclaims. "Come on, Gloria, what do you say?"

Even if she bought enough to last for two weeks, she could not easily hide the packets from Steve in a motel room. Besides, if they were together twenty-four hours a day for fourteen days straight, when would she be able to snort? *Could I go fourteen days straight without snorting? Yes, sure, but right now the thought is unbearable.*

"Didn't I tell you Tony asked me to work at the restaurant

during break and I said I would?" An inspired lie; she'll call her brother as soon as Steve leaves and tell him she wants to work over break.

Steve's body tenses in her arms. "No, you did not tell me, and you could have shared that bit of information sooner." He backs away and runs a hand through his hair. "You don't need the money. Last I knew, you had three grand in your savings. Damn, Gloria, we could use some time together away from here."

Think fast, placate him, and say whatever he needs to hear, just end this and get him out the door. "I know, and we will, but let's wait until summer. The lake's better than the ocean, freshwater, no crowds, and you won't have to drive two days straight."

During the past six months, half of Gloria's three grand has gone up her nose. Working two weeks for Tony plus tips will buy her another six months' worth.

"I don't know about you waiting tables over break," Steve says. "You look worn-out. I'll bet you've lost five pounds. And what's up with your nose?"

Gloria drops her head, her breath catching in her throat. "It's bigger, isn't it?"

"What?" Steve laughs. "It's red and running. Have you caught a cold? Come over here—you are so cute." Steve opens his arms and Gloria steps into them.

"I probably did. Honey, I'm sorry I forgot to tell you about working. I was thinking I'd save enough for a down payment on a car. I know you don't like me taking the bus. I'll make the next two weeks special right here at home, cook elegant dinners, clean the house, be a regular Martha Stewart." *Will you leave now, please!*

GLORIA EMPTIES the remainder of the heroin onto a stoneware coaster and taps the packet bottom. She snorted a line half an hour ago, but it didn't get her high enough to forget the aches in her joints, her score on the exam, and lying to Steve. She doesn't know how much is in a packet, but when she first started using, a packet would last a week. Of course, she only did it once or maybe twice a week then, and now she's up to once a day. She rolls a dollar bill tightly, sticks one end in her right nostril, snorts the last of her stash and lies back on the couch.

How did this start, she wonders, and why? Freshman year, finals week, economics exam the next morning, and she couldn't stay awake. Her roommate gave her some pills. "Everyone in the dorm uses bennies," she said. They worked— wow, did they ever. She not only stayed awake all night but was focused, motivated, sure she'd ace the exam. Kept using bennies until Steve, coming down was so bad. Then . . . last October used them again . . . and right after midterms, working night shift at Amelio's, Steve left for a week, training up north . . . couldn't sleep after stopping the bennies . . . after closing one night, she, Tony, and Darryl stayed late talking, laughing. Tony said she looked beat, go home, get some sleep, and she told him she'd tried but couldn't . . . Tony left and Darryl put the little white packet, dinosaur stamped on the outside, on the table. She asked what it was. "China Cat," he said, and she said, "Cocaine," and he said, "Hell no, I wouldn't do that shit, you snort it, wanna try? It's natural from poppies *Papaver somniferum* . . . flower of sweet dreams."

GLORIA IS dreaming. The Parsons rep is interviewing her, and she can tell that he likes everything he has heard. He reaches inside his briefcase and removes a scholarship form. He pauses, clicks his pen, then says he almost forgot about the health history form. Gloria feels her joints begin to harden.

Has anyone in your family ever had or been treated for heart disease?

No, she answers, and her nose grows an inch. The man does not look up from the paper, and Gloria clamps her hand over her nose.

Is anyone in your family an alcoholic?

No, she answers, and her nose grows another inch, sliding out from between her fingers. The man checks off another box and still does not look up.

Are you currently using or have you ever used illegal drugs?

No, Gloria answers, and her nose shoots out a foot in length, poking the man just below his right eye. Gloria stands and tries to run from the room, but as soon as she takes a step, she is yanked backward. She lifts her arms and discovers strings tied to her wrists; she looks down and sees strings tied to her ankles. She tries again to flee the room, and then she hears laughter from above her head. When she looks up, she sees Darryl holding the hand strings and her mother dancing the strings attached to her feet.

"Gloria—Gloria?"

Someone is shaking her shoulder. Gloria opens her eyes and remembers she's at Megan's house.

"You were out like a light," Megan says. "Wish I could sleep so soundly. Everything go all right with Jake?"

Gloria sits up quickly and her head spins. She stretches out her legs; she had slept on her left one and she bounces her heel against the floor to drive out the prickles. "I fixed Sloppy Joes for dinner. He did his homework, we played a few games on his PlayStation, and he went to bed. He's a sweet kid."

Gloria doesn't mind sitting for Jake; she has never snorted at Megan's, and although she was still a bit high when she got here, there was never a question in her mind that she couldn't properly care for Jake.

Megan hands Gloria ten dollars; fifty a week, one packet a week. "Thanks, Gloria. You're the only sitter Jake actually likes—actually *tells* me how much fun he had with you. Are you and Steve planning a family?"

"That's a long way off," Gloria replies. However, this reminds her of the extra birth control pill she discovered on the thirty-first. She and Steve had not been intimate for a while, but were they on the night she missed that pill?

STEVE IS sitting in his recliner watching TV when Gloria comes home. He's wearing gray sweats, a Budweiser in his hand, a bowl of popcorn on the floor beside him. Gloria crosses the room and curls up in his lap, needing some comfort after the interview nightmare. *I am so lucky; he's strong, smart, hardworking, handsome, he loves me, and I don't deserve him.*

Gloria kisses his cheek and Steve ducks his head to the left, intent on the TV screen.

"What are you watching?"

"HBO. See, now that is totally Hollywood," Steve says, pointing his beer at the set.

Gloria looks up at the screen where Uma Thurman lies on the floor, face contorted, eyes fixed, blood leaking from her nose. "What's wrong with her?"

"Supposedly, she just overdosed from snorting heroin."

As John Travolta drags Uma toward a car, Gloria listens carefully to Steve's words.

"See, she used crack or something earlier, and if you don't know your drugs, you'd miss that. It's rare that someone dies from snorting heroin. Most likely a snorter who dies would fall asleep and choke to death on vomit. In our drug education unit they told us how hard it is to spot a heroin user. I mean weed makes you stupid, speed fucks you up and you look fucked up, but not heroin. Maybe if the person was naive about percentage and weight, had been drinking, doing other drugs, and was petite, like you, it might happen like that." Steve playfully rubs the top of Gloria's head. "Yeah, like a cop's wife would snort heroin."

"I don't know how you can watch this," Gloria says, rising from his lap. She is light-headed and her temples throb. "I'm getting a Coke and going to bed."

Gloria walks to the kitchen and peers around the door frame to watch the screen. Uma is now on the floor in another apartment. John rips open her blouse and paints a big red dot on her chest. Then he takes a hypodermic needle from a black case and plunges it into Uma's chest.

Gloria has left the kitchen before Uma bolts up screaming, needle protruding from her chest; she doesn't hear Steve howl with laughter.

SHE WILL quit the day spring break begins. She was going to quit today, but after spending half an hour in Professor Chaney's office, trying to convince him to let her retake the exam and failing to do so, she needed to snort. She needed to stop the hopelessness dragging her down, the feeling that she was a failure, so she stopped at Amelio's on the way home.

Gloria turns the packet over in her hand. There's a tombstone stamped on the front side. Darryl had said it was killer stuff, South American. She sits on the couch, taps out a line on the stoneware coaster, rolls a dollar bill, and snorts. Ten seconds, twenty, thirty, and Gloria slides off the couch, nausea shooting from her stomach into her throat. She begins crawling for the bathroom and vomits next to the recliner. *Lie still, lie still, no not on your back, you could choke to death.* She rolls to her side, panting. Ten minutes, twenty minutes, thirty, and she is able to stand. The nausea is gone, the pain is gone, and the sting of failure has disappeared in the promise of a bright tomorrow.

It was stronger than the stuff she had used before. The next day, Gloria cut the amount by half and she didn't vomit. By the seventh day she was down to a quarter because she was scared. After six months of using heroin, she is not snorting to get high anymore; she is snorting to stop the pain in her joints, the muscle spasms, the cramps, the sweating and chills, the insomnia and irritability.

GLORIA SETS a tray of dirty dishes on the conveyor and rushes to the ladies' room. She barely makes it in time. The other stall is occupied, and under normal circumstances she would wait until the woman left, but today is far from normal. This is her third day of spring break working at Amelio's, her third without snorting, and her period is two weeks late. The diarrhea started yesterday morning and it kept her running to the bathroom half the night.

Gloria washes her hands and hurries back to the kitchen. She clips up her orders and notices Darryl giving her a sidelong glance. "You're sweating," he whispers.

"I know." Gloria grabs a napkin from the cart and wipes her forehead. "I can handle it."

By 3:00, Gloria's joints ache and her back spasms every ten minutes. Thank God Tony's not in today. Two more hours then home to keep the promise she made to Steve about making spring break "special." There are only a few customers in the restaurant and they've been served. Gloria goes to the kitchen and takes a beer from the refrigerator.

"Want me to cook you a burger," Darryl says. "You haven't eaten all day and you look like shit."

Gloria sips the beer and leans against the counter. "I feel like shit, and there's only one thing that can make it all better, and it's definitely not a burger."

⌒

GLORIA PLACES the pan of frozen lasagna she'd taken from Amelio's into the oven. She unwraps the loaf of garlic bread and sets it in the sink to thaw. She and Steve fought last night. He had wanted sex and she put him off claiming she was coming down with the flu. Steve told her she had better not go into work today. She felt like screaming, *If I don't keep my hands busy, if I don't keep moving, if I stand still for too long, I'll snort a line—I ache all over, I can't concentrate, and on top of that, I might be pregnant!*

Her sleep was fitful, disturbed by the same interview nightmare she had a few weeks ago: her nose growing out of control, the strings on her arms and legs pulled by Darryl and her mother. However, this time, as she stood to run from the room, Steve appeared with a pair of scissors in his hand.

Now, sitting in her kitchen, she tries to draw in the familiarity of this room to comfort her mind. *There is the toaster, there is the microwave, there is Boston fern hanging in the window, here on the table is my camera.* She lifts the camera and begins shooting, but it doesn't work, it does not stop time from spinning out of control. Her brain flashes images of Big Tony in Amelio's kitchen, staring at his shoes, *I told you before, she's visiting your aunt Connie;* Tony Junior putting a bandage on her knee, *You can cry for Mommy all you want, she ain't here;* the kids at school, *Liar, liar, pants on fire, nose is longer than a telephone wire;* the Parsons rep sitting in a chair, Parsons School appearing behind him, and both receding fast into a concrete tunnel; her mother standing in the kitchen singing, *I'm a little teapot short and stout, here is my handle here is my spout, when I get all steamed up then I shout, just tip me over, pour me out.*

"Like mother, like daughter," Gloria shouts, throws the camera across the room, then sobs into her hands.

STEVE ENTERS the kitchen holding a dozen red roses in front of his face. He peeks out from behind the flowers. "Still mad?"

Gloria shakes her head.

"I'm sorry," he says, and sits beside her at the table. "You worked eight hours a day at the restaurant over break then came home and made things so nice. I appreciate everything you did, and I'm proud of you for doing so well in school." He places the flowers in Gloria's lap.

Gloria touches the velvety blooms and her eyes and nose sting with emotion. "Thank you, honey, they're so beautiful. I'm going to put them in water right now."

Reaching for a vase, Gloria feels a rush of wet warmth between her legs. She hurries to the bathroom, pulls down her slacks, and finds her panties filled with blood. As she sits on the commode, spasms begin radiating through her abdomen. Gloria bends at the waist and moans.

"Are you okay, babe? You've been in there awhile."

"I started my period. I'll be out in a minute." After five minutes the rhythmic cramping stops. Gloria rises shakily; she splashes her face with cold water and rinses her panties in the sink. *Don't look, just flush and go to Steve; he's waiting for you.* Gloria can't resist looking: a bright red mass floats in the pink-stained water like a tiny rosebud.

GLORIA FILLS a vase with water and tears the preservative packet open with her teeth. She stirs the water with a long handled wooden spoon until the powder dissolves. She arranges the roses one by one and places the vase on the table, then sits across from her husband.

"I've been thinking about your graduation," Steve says. "I mean, what will happen after you graduate. Have you thought about what you'd like to do with your degree?"

"Not lately."

Steve leans forward and takes her hand. "I like this city, my beat, and I like the neighborhood. I introduced myself to the new couple next door, Alex and Jane Williams. They said it was nice to know a cop lives on the street. But hey, I can get a job just about anywhere, and you're smart, Gloria, really talented. So if you get an offer from some big city outfit, I'd move. I would do that for you. Or we can stay here, you don't have to decide right away."

"Maybe I'll work for Tony awhile after graduation."

"Okay." Steve shrugs.

"And maybe we could think about starting a family."

Steve, rising from his chair with a whoop, lifts Gloria from her chair. As he twirls her about, Gloria grabs a rose from the vase, holds it under her nose, and inhales the heady sweet scent.

Pri·de

The Fourth Sin
Pride

REMEMBER THE Bugs Bunny cartoon where Elmer Fudd is hunting Bugs when an Acme Theater truck drives by, hits a bump, and dozens of hats fall out the back? The hats are carried by the wind, and they land on Elmer's and Bugs's heads. Each time a new hat lands, their personalities change to match the hat. That's what I'm reminded of watching my brother Frankie, who is wearing the hat Mom sent him last Christmas. The hat is black corduroy, and on the front is a gold eagle, wings spread above the words:

VIET VET AND PROUD OF IT

Frankie can't keep his hands off the hat. He fingers the brim and talks about his new Chevy pickup. He pushes it back on his crown and describes the stream where he caught twelve brook trout last week. He moves it forward and says he's getting too old to cut trees for a living. He takes off the hat and silently stares at the insignia.

During the past half hour Frankie has said more than I've

heard him say in the past twenty-five years. We're sitting out-side at a picnic table in my backyard on Lantern Hill Lane. There are four of us: Frankie, my husband Alex, my husband's brother Pete, and me. It's a hot and humid July late afternoon in south Lansing, and we're halfway through a cold case of Heineken.

Frankie sets the hat firmly on his head, opens another beer, and says, "Dad's a tough old bird."

Yesterday my father went into cardiac arrest. The Har-rison County sheriff hiked two miles into the woods east of Small's Creek and tacked a note on my brother's cabin. Frankie rarely comes "downstate," and he refuses to have a telephone.

I was in the Intensive Care lounge this morning when I heard his boots in the corridor. The heaviness in my chest light-ened with each step. He came around the corner with sleeves rolled up on his freckled forearms. He hugged me, his stiff red beard chafing my ear. "Janey bug. Is Mom inside? How's he doing?"

"Better, but Frankie, he looks—"

I bit my lip. I couldn't tell him how white and small Dad seemed in that room, hooked up to blinking, hissing machines. Frankie took my hand in his loosely. His calluses scraped my knuckles as we walked in together.

"Hey, Buddy," he said, and leaned down to hug Dad and kiss his cheek.

"You're wearing the hat." Dad smiled, his eyes watery, and I sat abruptly in one of two plastic chairs. The only time I had seen my father and brother embrace was the night Frankie re-turned from Vietnam. I had never seen my father cry, and I covered my mouth, turned my head.

I recalled the day Frankie ran crying into the kitchen, his nose bloodied. Some kid had chased him all the way to our house, then stood on our front lawn yelling, "Chicken." Dad thumped the side of Frankie's head and said, "Boys don't cry." He told Frankie to go outside and finish the fight, make him proud, or he'd get a worse beating from him.

"I told your mother you might not want to wear it."

Mom tugged the back of Frankie's shirt. "I've always been proud of you, Franklin Williams."

Frankie would have made any parents proud. He became a Little League standout, his report cards glowed with praise, he was vice president of student council, lettered in three sports, played in the high school jazz band, was a member of the Honor Society and the debate team. He had scholarship offers from six universities before he enlisted.

I was not a great student, nor was I musically inclined. Words did not roll easily from my mouth as they did from Frankie's. The best I could do to make my parents proud was to marry well and be a good mother.

My mother had bought Frankie's hat through a mail-order catalog. I was surprised for two reasons: first, she has a phobic distrust of catalogs, and second, not a single member of our family ever talks about Frankie's Vietnam service. Frankie wouldn't allow it when he first came home, and in the years that followed, as we heard the truth from veterans, doctors, and poets, we would suffer in silence rather than breach the wall Frankie had built around his private horrors.

I stood in her living room as she lifted the hat from the box as if it was a shadow in her hands. She turned to me, her entire face drawn into a question mark. I didn't know whether she was expecting me to comment or if she had simply surprised herself. "Jane," she said finally, "isn't it about time? I think it's time we let him know we're proud of him for going over there."

⌇

NOVEMBER 1967, ten past nine o'clock on a Friday night, I was sixteen, wearing a pink angora sweater, a white wool skirt, and a pink velvet ribbon in my hair, waiting for my date. Dad was watching *Man from U.N.C.L.E.,* and Mom and Frankie's wife, Marcia, sat at the dinner table drinking coffee. Michelle, my month-old niece, slept with her cheek pressed to Marcia's chest. The front door swung open and Frankie stepped into the lighted entryway.

We were not expecting him. He had not phoned from the airport. After seven months of bargains offered in prayer, of creases worried into Mom's face, of Dad flinging his morning paper to the floor—there he was, striding across the room. Marcia's face turned, like slow motion, her eyes closing, pushing tears to her chin. Frankie kissed her, kissed his daughter's forehead, and we moved in stuttered cries and steps to embrace him.

Marcia told me, years later, after their divorce, the story he told her about that homecoming night. There were protesters at the airport throwing tomatoes. She told me how Frankie had cleaned tomato seeds and red stains off his uniform in a gas station while the cab waited. She said Frankie told her they had spit on him too, and to please never tell the old man.

THE SUN is nearly down, and Frankie has worn that hat all day. He puts his arm around my shoulder and says again, "Yep, a tough old bird. Just like the Duke." He removes the hat and sets it on the table. "Dad and I used to love those old westerns. Don't have a television now."

Frankie watched hour after hour of TV in 1967 during the four months he and his family lived at our house. He would be in front of the set with a scotch on ice when I came home from school. At 4:00 he would turn off the TV and go to his room for a nap. The house grew quiet, despite the baby; all the women in Frankie's life cushioned him with silence. He had developed a mean streak, and his size, strength, and penetrating glare could make a state trooper think twice about hassling Frankie.

We were so grateful that he was alive. Even if this raw-nerved, sullen man was not the same Frankie that had gone to Vietnam, he was home, and if we waited, gave him enough time, he would come back to us all the way.

Mom always asked me to wake him for dinner because at that hour she was busy in the kitchen and Marcia was feeding the baby. The first time, I was not expecting his reaction, I couldn't jump away fast enough, and his right hand connected with my thigh. Frankie jolted upright, and when he realized he had not nodded off in a jungle foxhole, that I was not the enemy, and he saw my crumpled chin, teeth clenched over my bottom lip, he slammed his fist into the mattress. After that I learned to stand in the doorway and toss a pillow onto his back.

Three days later I was fresh from the shower, wrapped in a towel, Mom and Frankie whispering in the hallway when the bruise stopped them, a bright, ripe plum. I had worn it secretly, like a badge of honor. I wanted Frankie to be proud of me, to know I was not a snitch. When Mom asked me what had happened, I told her that I slipped on ice on the sidewalk. I looked up at Frankie, expecting the wink I had received so many times when we had innocently put one over on our parents. Frankie shook his head slowly, walked to his bedroom, and closed the door behind him.

FRANKIE CLOSED the door on many things after 1967, including the shoes my father had polished and waiting for him. He tried; he put in two years as vice president of Dad's company, suit and tie, nine to five.

I remember Mom standing in our driveway watching the U-Haul carry away her son, daughter-in-law, and granddaughter to the Upper Peninsula. "A farm, for God's sake," she whimpered. Dad watched through the living room window.

Frankie was back a year later, roaring up the drive on a Harley Sportster, divorced, his possessions strapped on the back in a duffel bag. He wouldn't tell us what had happened, but I knew, because I'd been at parties at his house before they moved. I had seen the friends he was cultivating, the bikers and boozers; I'd seen the circles under Marcia's eyes at 1:00 A.M., asking them please to keep the noise down, the baby was sleeping. She had told me Frankie needed the blaring music, the drunken laughter, to drown out the screaming in his head. I knew it was her idea to move to a farm to pull him out of the downward spin, and I knew it had not worked.

We were a stop-off, one night's rest before heading to Florida. The Harley was stolen on his third day in Miami. He found work on a fish boat, but it was seasonal. When he couldn't raise enough money for rent, he came back to Michigan, hair to his shoulders, a gold cross in his ear.

Although Frankie lived at Mom and Dad's, he was rarely home. He kept ridiculous hours and made phone calls in the middle of the night. He took a job working the line at Oldsmobile, which rankled Dad to the point that arguments finally drove Frankie to an apartment on Lansing's West Side. His second marriage lasted eight months. Frankie's bride was twelve years his junior. They married one week after they met at the Jackson Motor Speedway. My mother has never forgiven that woman for telling her about the night that Frankie put a gun in his mouth.

After the divorce, Frankie bought a tent and a kerosene heater. He camped in the middle of two hundred acres Dad owns in Harrison County. He worked in a sawmill where he lost his left eye in a staple gun accident. With the insurance payment added to his savings, he was able to buy eight wooded acres of his own. He started cutting for a lumber company, and last year moved out of the tent into a log cabin he built with trees he had cleared from his land.

MY BROTHER-IN-LAW Pete pulls a bag of weed from his pocket and rolls a joint. Frankie keeps touching that hat, running his fingers along the corduroy. This is the first time Frankie and Pete have met. Peter is visiting from Canada and he doesn't know better. Watching Frankie stare at the insignia, Pete passes him the joint and asks about the war.

I flinch—I can already hear Frankie's fist pound the redwood, but this doesn't happen. He puts the hat back on his head and says he was a helicopter door-gunner in 'Nam. Frankie takes a hit; I hear him suck air through his teeth, the sudden stop as his tongue covers the space between his lips.

He passes the joint to my husband Alex and says that fine drugs once saved his life over there. He says he was on a recon mission when they flew over a field of poppies. Frankie laughs about pleading with the pilot to set down long enough to snap a pocketful of pods. And he keeps touching that hat. I think he has forgotten that I'm sitting beside him.

He says there was a temple at the edge of the poppy field, and they landed with shotguns cocked.

"Didn't you carry M-16s?" Pete asks.

Frankie tells him for close-up combat, a shotgun was best, that the Cong would get zonked on dope, slither around the jungle like snakes, and you'd have to hit them in the head or the heart using an M-16, otherwise they'd keep on coming. A shotgun would blow a hole right through them.

"We didn't need the guns," Frankie says, turning the hat backward on his head, "the temple was deserted."

He goes on to explain that inside he found a bowl of temple ball hash, and he popped two before getting back in the chopper and strapping on the gunner harness.

"The balls kicked in while we were over water. Man, I started melting, slipped right out of the goddamn seat into open air."

Frankie removes the hat, dents in the top with the side of his hand and then pushes it out from underneath. He says the harness kept him from falling, but there he was, dangling out in the sky like a kite tail, so peaceful and happy, he says, weightless in a blue vacuum.

"I managed to pull myself back in the chopper when I realized we were coming into camp. I'd been in my tent about fifteen minutes stretched out on my cot. The C.O. came in and hauled my ass outside. He points at the side of the chopper and says, 'Fuck me gently. Am I talking to a ghost?' "

Frankie pushes the brim back on his forehead, smiles, and he says the C.O. pointed to a line of machine-gun fire that ran straight through the middle of the gunner door where Frankie would have been sitting if not for the hash.

"Holee-shit!" Pete squeals.

Frankie removes the hat and rubs his forehead. "You expect it, you're ready for it in the choppers and in the jungle. So they'd get you when you least expected. Couldn't trust anyone, not even the kids."

He stops and turns to me. Alex and Pete glance at me too, briefly, then tip their beers. Tree frogs chirp through the protracted silence. Off in the bushes fireflies flicker and dim like small towns at night viewed from an airplane window flying into Detroit. Frankie does not break his stare, and I realize that this may be the first time he has talked about Vietnam. It may be because of Dad's brush with death, it may be the humid,

Michigan summer night, it may be because Alex and Peter are Canadians, or it may be the hat. Regardless, I know that if I stay, he will remain as silent as his stare, as still as his sister's pride. I say good night, walk into the house, and close the door behind me.

Friday's Child
Is Loving and Giving

I ONCE had a sister in Vietnam. Wait, that's not how I should start . . . [Stop] . . . [Record] My name is Rebecca Lovejoy. I'm making this recording to tell the story of my unexpected journey into the past and how it changed my life forever. I bought a lovely journal in which I intend to transcribe this tape, but for now, it's the quickest and easiest way because my hands are full.

When did this all begin? With Dad—yes, three years ago my father died from cirrhosis of the liver. I never really knew him. He had left Mom and me when I was young. He died in Indianapolis, where he had been living and drinking himself to death. Dad was a Vietnam veteran, a casualty of war thirty years later.

After the American Legion sent to my mother those few things he had left behind, Mom mailed me a photograph. There was a letter too. She wrote, *Rebecca, I didn't know about the child. Even though I've been happily remarried for a long time, this breaks my heart.*

The photo shows my father in Vietnam, before I was born.

He is dressed in fatigues and wearing sunglasses. He is sitting in a chair with his arm around a petite, beautiful Vietnamese woman. He is holding a little girl on his lap. She has short black hair that shines in the sunlight. She's wearing a red blouse and blue shorts. On the back of the photo is written: *My daughter Tuyet, Kim, and me, Saigon, 1969.*

Oh, that wailing's going to be on the tape.

"Mommy's coming, Ryan." [Stop]

[RECORD] WE are a bit concerned about Ryan. At age ten months, he has not tried to roll over or sit up. Our pediatrician said not to worry, some children are just slower to start than others are. But I worry over everything where Ryan is concerned. I never thought we would be blessed with a child; Bill is sterile and . . . I'm getting off track here. [Stop]

[Record] Bill and I had tried to get pregnant for a few years, and after consulting a specialist, we found out Bill was sterile. Just after learning that news, I received the photo from my mother, and I decided to go to Vietnam to find my half sister. I'm not sure why it hit me so strongly, the urge to go. I guess I was feeling sort of lost and drifty, Bill and I clinging to each other too much to make sure the other was okay.

During my childhood, I wanted a sister more than anything. I kept pestering Mom, "When can I have a sister?"

"When donkeys fly," she would say.

Or I would say, "If I had a sister, I wouldn't be bored."

Mom would say, "If a frog had wings, he'd save his butt a lot of bumping." Mom has always been a card, but now that I think of it, I guess she felt grounded, not knowing what happened to Dad and waiting years for a divorce.

Then Mom sent the photo, and I found out I had a half sister all along. I wanted to make up for lost time; I wanted to get away from Lantern Hill Lane and the empty room we had planned on using as a nursery.

Bill was gently not keen on the idea. He played the devil's advocate. "Becky, honey," he said, "what do you know about Vietnam? It's on the other side of the world. Do you think the Vietnamese people will welcome you? That war is still an old and angry wound. How are you going to find your sister among the millions of people in Saigon? Even if you manage to find her, how will you communicate? How do you think she's going to feel about meeting the daughter of the father who left her?"

What did I know about Vietnam? A study unit in high school history class with staggering numbers and shameful details about Mylai and napalm. And the movies I saw during my teens—oh, the movies: *Apocalypse Now, Platoon, Born on the Fourth of July, Full Metal Jacket.* I watched them all, eager to put my father into that scenery so I could understand what made him unable to stay with Mom and me, and forgive . . . [Stop]

[Record] I told Bill I will tell my sister that Dad left me too. [Stop]

[RECORD] SIX months have passed since my last recording—before I became a full-time mom, I could have completed the project in a few days. But I'm not in a hurry, and it's sort of fun to come back to the recorder and add a bit now and then. Ryan is sixteen months old now, his father's pride and his mother's joy. He is small for his age, which, of course, worries me. He is walking now, but is not yet steady on his feet—and he won't walk around barefooted! He cries the minute his bare feet touch the ground. He has always startled easily, but now he also has become very sensitive to loud noises. Last week an ambulance went by on Cedar Street. Ryan went bonkers— screaming, crying, and he would not let me pick him up. He toddled into his room and hid in the closet. When we go in for his eighteen-month checkup, I'm going to ask the pediatrician to check his hearing. [Stop]

[Record] I just realized I should explain that Ryan is as much a part of my journey into the past as was my desire to find my sister, Tuyet. Because of Ryan, the journey was transformed from dark despair into a bright promise of love and hope.

Where did I leave off last time? Okay, I convinced Bill that this was something I just had to do. I searched the Internet and found a U. S. Consulate General Office in Ho Chi Minh City, the former Saigon. To make a long story short, after several e-mails back and forth, it was determined that my father had not registered Tuyet as his daughter, so there was no documentation at the Consulate General for any child named Tuyet Bogard—Bogard was my maiden name. They advised me to attempt contacting several Vietnamese government departments and various hospitals, but responses may take months.

Months—I couldn't bear months of waiting, so I got my passport, and on August 5, I boarded a plane at Detroit Metro Airport to begin the first leg of my long trip to Vietnam.

I was already exhausted by the time I landed in Los Angeles. Of course, my thoughts during the whole flight were of Tuyet: Is she married and is she a mother? Is her favorite color green like mine? Are lilacs her favorite flowers? Do they have lilacs in Vietnam? Does she like ghost stories as much as I do? Does she wear a size six dress and size eight shoes? Will she agree to meet me? Will she be scared or angry? Does she walk like my father, as I do—the only thing I can remember of him except for his turquoise blue eyes?

"What Ryan? What is it you want? Can you point to it? Ow, don't pinch Mommy." [Stop]

[RECORD] WE celebrated Ryan's second birthday last week. I bought a digital camera and I use the picture of him blowing out the candles as my screen saver. Well, his dad had to help him blow them out, and then Ryan stuck both hands into the middle of the cake. Bill said, "That's my boy—dig in."

When I got a washcloth to clean him up, Ryan threw his arms around my neck and squeezed so tight I had to gasp for air. Ryan needs to grab on tight to something when he's excited. He can never get enough of his mom, and I gladly give him all the love I have to give.

Oh, and his hearing is fine, but he is prone to ear infections. He is a little whirlwind, never sitting still to play with one toy for more than a few minutes. He's still not sleeping through the night, but that's partly my fault, I'm sure, because I can't stand to hear him cry, and I love to snuggle him! I told the pediatrician about his not sleeping. I didn't have to tell him about

Ryan's activity level—he was into everything in the exam room, opening cupboards and drawers, ripping the paper on the exam table, and not sitting still for the doctor to examine him. I had to hold him, and he screamed the whole time. The nurse gave me some pamphlets on parenting when we left. Now Bill takes over mostly on weekends so I can catch up on my sleep.

Ryan wants me to join in on everything he does. Bill's nickname for Ryan is Mom Bird because Ryan constantly yells, "Mom, Mom, Mom," and he looks like a chirping baby bird in the nest. I'm going to enroll him in a preschool class at MSU this fall where he can burn off some of that energy in play with kids his age. Maybe that will give me time to finish this tape. [Stop]

[Record] I was talking about the plane ride. Well, I came up with more questions—dozens of them during the thirteen-hour flight. I remember realizing when the plane was an hour away from Hong Kong that it was still August 6 back in Michigan. I couldn't remember being in the day of August 6, and it only lasted for a few hours in the air, I think. I whispered to myself, *I'm so far from home.* But the farther from home, the closer I was to meeting my sister, Tuyet.

I kept my face practically glued to the window all the way from Bangkok to Ho Chi Minh City, anxious for my first glimpse of Vietnam. Oh, I met another American woman on the plane. She stopped in the aisle to say hello and ask where I was from. I told her I lived in Lansing, Michigan, and she said she was from Minneapolis. She opened her purse and pulled out a photograph. "This is why I'm going to Vietnam, to adopt my daughter." The woman handed me the photo and she kept talking. She was giddy with excitement. "There is a group of us here, we are all adopting from the same orphanage in Soc Trang," she said.

The woman's excitement seemed contagious and I nearly reached for Tuyet's picture. Then I remembered Dad was also in the photo, and although I had precious few memories of my father, I didn't want a stranger passing judgment on his character.

I gave her my congratulations and turned back to the window. As Vietnam came into view, I thought about how different my father's expectations and fears must have been from mine the first time he saw this land. [Stop]

[RECORD] I am determined to get my story recorded. Ryan is three years old now and he takes up almost all my time. The recommendations in the pamphlets on parenting do not work with Ryan. You know, when you're with a child every day, you get used to the way they act, move, sleep or not sleep, talk or try to talk. Ryan was not saying more than a few words, at least any that made sense. It was at the MSU preschool class that I realized how different he was compared to children his age. I had to stay the whole time on the first day because Ryan screamed when I tried to leave. The second day he screamed too, but the teacher said it was best for me to leave. When I returned an hour later, she said she was sorry, but Ryan could not stay in her class. He was too disruptive; he took toys from other children, drew on other children's paper, and would not listen to instructions. She said the school would refund my money, and she suggested I take Ryan to Dr. Linda Connors, a neurologist. [Stop]

[Record] Dr. Connors prescribed a low dosage of Dexedrine for Ryan. She said he showed signs of ADD, Attention Deficit Disorder, but she also made an appointment for us with a geneticist to cover all the bases, as she put it. Since he's been taking Dexedrine, he has calmed down so much. He has proudly said four word phrases and stopped rushing around long enough to enjoy playing with a toy. [Stop]

[Record] I had to rewind to find out where I left off, which was arriving in Vietnam. Hot and humid! Summers can be sticky in Michigan but desertlike compared to Ho Chi Minh City. I remember feeling envious of the small group of Americans who were there to adopt children. A man was waiting for them with a sign written in English. They stood with him while someone got their luggage from the conveyor. The conveyor belt was small, and I seemed to tower over the little old ladies who kept elbowing me to the back of the crowd. My desire to be polite to a people I was sure already despised me, or likely found me laughable, kept down my urge to reach over their heads and grab my suitcase. Now that I actually had my feet in my sister's home country, I felt like racing to her.

The taxi driver spoke English, at least enough to get me to the hotel where I had made a reservation. However, I must say he spoke chiefly with his horn. Everyone honked—taxis, motorcycles, cars, cyclos, and people on bikes. And there were no traffic lights. Everyone moved through the mess in spurts and stops.

After I checked in, I called Bill to let him know I had arrived. Then I got out the photo of Tuyet and the list of places the Consulate General suggested I try and placed them on the bed. My treasure and my treasure map. I changed into a clean dress and went to the front desk with my list.

The man politely told me that these places were closed for the day. He pointed to his watch. "Dinner time," he said, and asked if I would like something to eat. He recommended a restaurant a few blocks away. Nearly as soon as I stepped out the door, a group of children gathered around me. They held up postcards, fans, and maps. "Only a dollar for postcard, one dollar for map, one dollar for fan," they said. Their English was far better than the cab driver's. At first I tried to ignore them, but I couldn't because we were packed together. The streets and sidewalks were jammed with people, with booths with trinkets for sale, and bicycles everywhere.

A young boy tugged my arm and asked, "Where you want to go, I can get you there." I told him the name of the restaurant, and he took my hand, then proceeded to push his way through the crowd. The little old ladies that had elbowed me a few hours earlier at the airport laughed and shook their fingers at the boy.

At the restaurant door, eager to get inside, I pulled out my cash and handed him a dollar. "Don't show all your money, lady," he hissed, and glanced around at the people seated on short stools at one-table sidewalk cafés. "They will take it from you."

After I had eaten, he was still there, along with about a dozen other kids. One said, "You have money to eat in restaurant, you can buy postcard, only one dollar."

"Ryan—no, no—put that down. Oh, I didn't mean to scare you, honey. Ryan, please give that to Mommy, you'll break—" [Stop]

⌒

[RECORD] I know something is wrong with Ryan. He talks all the time, to anyone who will listen, mostly Bill and me because it's hard to take him out in public. When I ask him a question, he will immediately answer, but it's not the right answer. It's even hard at home sometimes. Twice now when we've had unexpected company—one of Bill's coworkers and his wife, then a friend from high school in Lansing visiting her parents—Ryan seemed to be happy. Of course, he talked nonstop, but he did not misbehave. Both times, after our company left, Ryan went through two days of destroying his toys and anything else that he could break. He had no release in his diaper for twenty-four hours, he wouldn't eat, and he barely slept.

In his gentle moments I know he wishes he could be different. He will touch my face softly and hug me. Oh, and he draws so well now—really, better than I can draw. He drew a picture with crayons of a dog running through a field that is so wonderful, I framed it and hung it on our kitchen wall.

We drove to Ann Arbor for the appointment Dr. Connors made with a geneticist. Five months and we're still waiting.

Waiting—I sure did a lot of that in Vietnam: waiting hours in government offices and hospital corridors, hours filling out forms, hours and hours waiting while someone checked records, only to be told they would take my name and get back to me. I gave the hotel phone number to a dozen or more people, and seven days passed by with me sitting in that hotel room, certain the phone would ring any minute with news of my sister.

On the eighth morning I woke at 5:00 A.M. and couldn't get back to sleep, so I decided to go for a walk. By this time I had learned that the city was safe, except for pickpockets, or motorcyclists who would grab items from Americans riding in rickshaws. I had learned that most of the people were living in poverty, and that they were commonly disinterested in me except for what I was willing to pay for goods or services. And that despite the poverty, the noise, and pollution, the people were peacefully engaged in the business of living, flowing through each day like the muddy water of the Saigon River.

Oh, it was lovely, quiet and amber-colored. Two boys were playing badminton in the street. On the sidewalks, men played cards at small tables and families were huddled together sleeping. I admit to staring at every sleeping face of a woman close to my age. Could she be Tuyet? Would her skin still be as fair as in the photo? Would her features bear any trace of my father?

I wandered into Cholan, the Chinese district, where people were already setting up for the markets to open. I had to walk around a square-shaped hole where a woman was dipping a bucket to wash the sidewalk in front of her stall. Another woman carrying a basket of vegetables on her head stopped to wash them in the hole.

A rickshaw driver passed me with a dozen live ducks tied together. In front of a store filled with 1950s style evening gowns, three half-naked children were gutting a huge carp. The scent of incense was very strong and rose in plumes from pagodas. I stopped in front of one to admire its bright and ancient architecture. There was an old man nearby with dozens of caged finches. "Five for a dollar," he said. "Take inside and let go to carry your prayers to the gods." He fluttered his hands and fingers high into the air, smiling and laughing. I bought five birds and released them inside the pagoda along with my prayers to find my sister.

When I got back to the hotel, the man at the front desk greeted me. He said, "You do not go out much. You should enjoy our beautiful city in the sunshine or see the countryside."

I told him I was expecting an important phone call. He smiled indulgently and said he would write down any message for me, Mrs. Lovejoy. Then he brought out several brochures and fanned them out on the counter. "Cu Chi Tunnels and War Remnants Museum are popular to Americans," he said. I didn't mean to, but I frowned at the color photos of war planes and people crawling through the maze of tunnels once used by the Viet Cong. The man quickly gathered them together and said I would most enjoy a sightseeing trip to the Mekong Delta, he would arrange everything.

I'm glad I took the trip because I may never have found out about my sister if I had not gone.

⌒

OUR PLANS and dreams for Ryan's future had to be adjusted to meet the needs of our special son. The geneticist informed us that Ryan has FASE, Fetal Alcohol Syndrome Effects. We were told his birth mother drank enough alcohol during her pregnancy to damage Ryan's brain. At age five we can expect him to take naps, follow one instruction, help

Mommy, sit still for ten to fifteen minutes, and engage in parallel play.

It took three hours by bus to reach the Mekong River. Until we were out of the city and suburbs, everytime the bus stopped, people would knock on the windows, showing us food and drinks for sale. Once we were into the countryside, the scenery was beautiful. We passed mango trees and banana plants and fields of rice. Women wearing conical bamboo hats bent over, transplanting rice seedlings by hand. At the river I transferred to a narrow boat that motored through a floating marketplace. The only thing I bought was a small watermelon—isn't that silly? Well, I knew one boat was selling watermelons because the vines were growing on tall poles. It was a hot day and the watermelons looked so delicious.

We got off the boat and had to wait half an hour for the bus to return. I walked to a grassy hill and sat down with my watermelon. Then I realized I had nothing that could cut open the fruit, and I lay my head on top of it and cried. Of course, I was not crying over the watermelon, but rather the realization that my grand plan to find Tuyet was as foolhardy and poorly thought out as buying the watermelon.

"Chewing gum," a voice said. "You want to buy some chewing gum?" I raised my head to see a teenage girl standing over me. Her clothes were worn thin and her feet were dirty. When she saw my tears, she sat down beside me and touched my arm. She asked me why I was crying, and I blubbered out the whole story to this poor girl: the photo of Tuyet and my father, flying to Vietnam from Michigan, getting turned away from place after place with no information on my sister, waiting all day by the telephone.

She said, "There is no place here for mother raising child without father. You want to find out about your sister, go to the orphanages." I wanted to kiss her, but only a polite handshake is appropriate in Vietnam. I bought two packages of gum, gave her the watermelon and an extra dollar with my gushing thanks. As I walked away she called after me, "Take gifts for the officials and the children."

As I recall, there were four orphanages close to Ho Chi Minh City. Anyway, after I had returned from the Mekong Delta trip, I hurried to the markets, where I bought clothing, brushes, blankets, toys, flowers, and candy. I remember it was on a Friday that I got into a taxi with my bags of gifts to go to the first orphanage. The drive took about half an hour, and on the way I held onto Tuyet's photo like a charm. I can't remember feeling such a mix of anticipation, excitement, awkwardness, and fear since I prepared for my first junior high school dance. Did Tuyet go to school dances? Did she have two left feet like me?

The cab pulled into a driveway and up to a long narrow building. As I got out of the cab, several older children and a few elderly people waved to me from the veranda of the building. The receptionist spoke English well, and after I explained why I was there, she ushered me into a small room. The room was decorated with a large photograph of Ho Chi Minh and flags of Vietnam and the Vietnamese Communist Party.

Mr. Nguyen, the director, asked me to sit down please, and I did, holding the bags in one hand and the picture of Tuyet in the other. I wanted to show him that photo and blurt out my story, but I reminded myself to stay calm and be polite. I gave

Mr. Nguyen a bouquet of sweetheart roses and a box of Swiss chocolates, and thanked him for seeing me.

He asked how he could help, and I placed the photo before him on the desk. "This is my father and my half sister, Tuyet," I said. "I didn't know I had a sister until last year when my father died. You can see on the back is written, 'My daughter Tuyet, Kim, and me, Saigon, 1969.' I've checked with the U.S. Consulate General, the hospitals in Ho Chi Minh City, and several government offices." I paused, wondering if I should repeat to Mr. Nguyen what the girl on the Delta told me about single mothers in Vietnam. I did not need to tell him.

"Do you know what 'Tuyet' means?" he asked. Then he told me my sister's name is Snow White. A name befitting a princess, I thought, and that wishing well song from the Disney film popped into my head: I'm wishing for the one I love to find me today.

Mr. Nguyen tapped the end of his pen on the desk, and he asked if I knew the mother's family name. I said no, and my heart sank as Mr. Nguyen shook his head slowly. If my father had not registered Tuyet as his daughter, it was doubtful there would be a record of her anywhere.

I felt tears burning under my eyelids, and then Mr. Nguyen said, "This was before my time. However, Mrs. Tran has been here over fifty years. It wouldn't hurt to show her this photograph; her memory is excellent. If you will please follow me to the nursery."

Such a small glimmer of hope, but enough to make me quickly grab the bags and follow Mr. Nguyen across the road to a small building. It was fully open to the outdoors, with only three walls. Mosquito netting for the platform beds was pulled back and fastened out of the way. A wide porch ran the length of the building and sheltered the entrance from the sun. There were several young women holding babies and an elderly woman rocking a baby in a bamboo cradle.

Mr. Nguyen approached the old woman and showed her the photo. They spoke in Vietnamese, so I couldn't understand, but my eyes stayed on Mrs. Tran, intent to catch a hint of recognition. And I saw it! I heard her say Tuyet.

The director turned to me and said Mrs. Tran told him she remembered the mother because they were born in the same northern village of Ninh Binh. Hoang Thi Kim was her name, and she brought Tuyet here around 1972. He asked me to wait in the nursery while he checked the records.

I was standing perhaps on the same floor where my sister once stood. Oh, how I wished I could talk to Mrs. Tran! She may have rocked Tuyet in that very cradle. She smiled at me, nodding her head and rocking the baby, back and forth, back and forth, as the minutes dragged by as I waited impatiently.

"Ryan, it is not time to go to the park. We go to the park at four o'clock. That's in one hour . . . one—" [Stop]

~

[RECORD] BILL used to get so impatient with Ryan. He would say, "He is a problem child. When is he going to grow up and act his age?" Now we know he's not a problem—he has a problem, static encephalopathy. His brain damage won't get any worse, but it won't get any better either. The only thing that will grow up will be his body. Bill thinks I'm overprotective of Ryan because I won't let him go to the park down the street by himself or spend the night at a friend's house from day care. I've told him it's too risky. Unless I'm by Ryan's side, he could get into big trouble . . . like last month when he smothered a guinea pig at school. He didn't mean to, he was excited and squeezed too tight.

Ryan can't remember what he got in trouble for yesterday. You would think he'd learn from his mistakes, but he can't. It's not that he doesn't understand the consequences, he does—he just can't make himself do what he knows he should do. [Stop]

[Record] I left off in the nursery, waiting for the director to return and wishing I could talk to Mrs. Tran. Then it occurred to me that one of the younger women might speak English and could act as an interpreter for me. But as I turned to ask, three couples entered the nursery with the receptionist. They spoke in French, and their eyes went from one baby to the next. The receptionist spoke to the nursery attendants, and one by one the French couples were given a baby. There were smiles and tears, laughter and cooing voices. The joy within the small room was nearly tangible.

"Mrs. Lovejoy." The director had come back and he was holding a file. I clenched my hands together, Would there be more photographs of Tuyet? Would there be the name and address of the family who adopted her? Would I finally be able to embrace my sister?

He opened the file and removed a newspaper article. This is what I remember him saying: "I am very sorry, you have come a long way and I do not have happy news. April 4, 1975,

an American Air Force transport taking 243 Vietnamese orphans to refuge in the United States burned shortly after take-
off from Saigon. It was the first in an airlift series to take many
hundreds of orphans to America to be adopted. Fifty of those
children came from this place. I am sorry, Mrs. Lovejoy, Tuyet
was on that plane." [Stop]

[Record] I can't possibly put into words how I felt after
hearing Mr. Nguyen tell me that Tuyet had died in 1975.
Perhaps when I have the time to transcribe this tape to my
journal, enough time will have passed being Ryan's mother.
Some children with FAS have facial features associated with
the syndrome, but Ryan's face is beautifully formed. That's
what I thought the first time I saw him.

I remember feeling like the air had been suddenly sucked
out of the nursery, amplifying all the sounds: the French couples speaking excitedly to one another, Mrs. Tran rocking the
cradle too fast; I thought, that's why the baby is crying; then a
monsoon rain drummed the roof. I wanted to cry on someone's
shoulder, but I couldn't. I started to raise my arms and realized
I was still holding onto the bags of gifts.

I held them out to Mr. Nguyen. "For the children," I said.
He took the bags and placed them on the floor, and then he led
me to a chair. He spoke to Mrs. Tran and she lifted the wailing
baby from the cradle and brought him to me. His hair was
pulled back into two little horns secured with rubber bands
and he wasn't wearing a diaper. I thought, This is the most
beautiful baby I have ever seen.

Mr. Nguyen asked if I had children in America, and I told
him no. He asked if I would like to be a mother. He said, "You

can adopt this baby, very easily. Because we are a government facility, I can provide all the necessary paperwork, visa for baby, everything you need. He is a good, strong baby and very handsome too, no?"

The rain stopped, sunlight poured onto the veranda, and Ryan fell asleep in my arms. [Stop]

[RECORD] THE logistics are boring stuff, it's enough to say that I brought Ryan home. The adoption was legal. However, since that time, twelve Vietnamese officials were accused of selling children to foreigners for adoption. They were acquitted at trial. I could have been more patient, I could have waited and adopted here at home, but I would not have Ryan, a gift of redemption to my father and a gift of love to us.

Well, that's the end of my story. At present, Ryan is taking Clonidine, and his vocabulary has tripled. He enjoys playing with his mom and dad, and for the first time in four years he is sleeping through the night. The key is to keep his routine predictable. We go to the same restaurants, the same stores, and the same play areas. It's easier for him to enjoy outings, as the environments become more familiar. Of course, he still has difficult days and we are prepared to leave when the signs first appear.

Transitions are difficult. We repeat what will happen next and where he is going, and this gives him time to prepare himself. My greatest challenge is that Ryan's not afraid of anything, strangers, heights, getting lost, or busy traffic.

After a week or so in Ho Chi Minh City, I learned to cross the streets by moving slowly and consistently, without pausing to think, because the drivers are gauging their paths by anticipating where you will be if you just continue moving. I will hold Ryan's hand tightly in mine until it is safe to let go.

The Fifth Sin
Lust

PRIVATE PROPERTY OF GEORGE C. SIMON
The Venus Journal

A S I L O O K back to the beginning and how innocently it started, I am troubled by how deep I have sunk.

I began watching her on the afternoon of Friday, June 10, when she moved into number 11 Lantern Hill Lane.

I had taken Dad's tray to his room: butter and bologna sandwich, corn chips, and iced tea. Then I sat at my desk to continue working on the paper I was determined to finish over summer sabbatical, a study on 3D laser scanning of fossils.

The persistent cry of a red-tailed hawk sent me searching through the closet for my binoculars; it's rare to see a hawk in the city. As I scanned the horizon, the sound of wheels turning into a driveway pulled my binoculars downward.

A plump feminine ankle emerged from the car, followed by thighs of powerful proportions that lifted her body upward and out. The sun shone through her gauzelike dress, outlining her enormous breasts, rounded stomach draping gracefully in rolls, her bulbous unrestrained buttocks, her golden bronze skin, and the intricate rows of plaited hair wrapped around her head. She raised her arms, and the sun striking her gold bracelets temporarily blinded me. When my eyes could focus again, I saw that she had placed her hands on the upper slope of her breasts and stood now looking at her new home. My fingers began trembling in that instant as I recognized her—the Willendorf Venus come to life!

I spent the night dreaming. I was an ant feeding on the sweet sap of an ancient, majestic pine. My feet became trapped in the sticky glob, and as I struggled, the sap swallowed my legs up to my knees. All night I struggled and sank deeper, until I was completely engulfed. Eons of time passed in my dream, until I finally awoke with the sun glowing through the orb of amber that encased me.

AT 8:30 A.M., Saturday, I was at my desk, research documents and photographs stacked in front of me, a blank sheet of paper in my typewriter. I heard the heavy slide of a moving van's doors and I was irresistibly drawn to the window. She stood in her doorway—filled the doorway—wearing shorts, sandals, and a sleeveless top. I watched, mesmerized, for an hour as she directed the movers. How many tender inches of skin from her toes to her head? How long would it take to measure the distance? How long would I have lingered at the window if not for the ungodly thumping coming from Dad's room?

He was marching again, naked but for the highly polished

black army boots and old dented helmet, bellowing, "Praise the Lord and pass the ammunition."

A week passed without writing a sentence, a week spent with binoculars pressed to my face, enduring the discomfort of a nearly constant state of erection. I spent hours at the window, desperate to catch another glimpse of her, knowing I was obsessing and helpless to stop. Why?

Whenever I examined a photo of fossilized ribs, I imagined Venus's ribs, cushioned by six inches of luxurious fat, expanding and contracting with her sacred breath, my fingers teasing those bronze folds, my hands filled with resilient flesh. And I would slide my hand furtively beneath the waistband of my sweatpants.

Within two weeks I had learned her pattern of comings and goings. She worked an eight-to-five job within walking distance, and drove somewhere each Thursday night at 7:45. Because of her schedule, 7:30 A.M. and 5:30 P.M. became the clock by which I set my life.

I would be up with the birds and stationed at my upstairs office window to watch her front door. Which was more enthralling, watching her emerge, head tucked, setting off down her front walk with determination to seize the day, or watching her move up the street more slowly at the end of it? I have never seen a woman walk as Venus does, with each step creating a small ripple at the ankle that spreads upward to her thighs, growing larger into her hips, where it breaks into rapturous waves thrusting her forward, only to begin anew.

I found while watching her walk that a Brahms lullaby would pop into my head. I began humming the song, twice a day matching the meter to her footsteps.

DAD WAS suspicious and cranky when I began going to his room on weekend mornings to watch the Weather Channel. He's a sports fanatic: ESPN, boxing matches, baseball games, tennis, every imaginable sport, including—good God—WWF wrestling. I needed to watch the Weather Channel because Venus was home on weekends. I would sit nervously in front of the TV, waiting for the local forecast, praying for sun. If the weather was fair on Saturday mornings, she worked outside. I can't describe the thrill of seeing her on her hands and knees digging in the earth, her buttocks swaying as she plants flowers and pulls weeds, crescent moons of sweat forming on her shorts beneath each enormous cheek. With the aid of my binoculars, I can be so close that her scent sticks to the back of my throat, antediluvian, the flavor of morels, earth, and smoke.

The TV is Dad's sole window on the world. Mother died when I was six, and Dad has not ventured out of Lansing since. After he retired from Oldsmobile, I invited him to come with me on fossil expeditions to Great Britain, Denmark, Greece, but eventually I gave up asking. One recent Saturday morning in July during a javelin championship being broadcast from New Zealand, I changed the channel and he threw a banana at my head. Consequently, I bought a small, portable TV.

Last winter Dad was diagnosed with dementia. Following the examination, the doctor spoke with me in private. He said my father's symptoms most likely were early signs of Alzheimer's, and that I should consider looking into a permanent care facility.

Somehow, Dad knew. He was quiet on the drive home, but once inside the house, he had plenty to say. "This is my house, the place I brought my bride after the war, the place you were born, and the place your mother died, and by Christ, I'm going to die here too. Remember, I raised you by myself and I can still take you down."

On Sunday, July 16, I caught a glimpse of sheets flapping in the breeze behind her house. It had rained the day before and I was sick with longing. So began the escalation of my obsession. I walked to the park at the end of Lantern Hill Lane, binoculars in hand, a middle-aged birdwatcher out for a Sunday stroll.

Once inside the park, I backtracked, slipped from tree to tree, darted behind her neighbor's backyard hedge, then crouched in the cover of a Norway pine at the edge of her yard, every fiber and every nerve yearning for the sight of Venus. She was wearing a housecoat, like Mother used to wear, the top two buttons undone, revealing a vast cleavage. The faraway, pristine memories of my mother should have sent me straight home. But as I watched Venus close her lips around clothespins and fasten her black undergarments to the line, I imagined myself stretched out on the damp earth beneath her, gazing up into the halo of hem and finding that her laundering had been thorough enough to leave nothing to my vivid imagination. At that ecstatic moment, Dad hollered from across the street, "George! George, where are you? Someone stole my boots, George!"

If I stayed, he would wander the entire neighborhood shouting, probably in nothing more than his helmet. As I turned to sneak away, a twig snapped underfoot. I lifted my head to peer through the branches and saw her eyes, bronze like an Abyssinian cat's, fixed on the pine. She tilted her head, and I swear she would have spotted me if Dad's bellowing, coming closer, had not caused her to turn toward the street.

Thereafter, my office became my blind, and the idea of a nursing home became more appealing.

AUGUST. THE dog days of summer have arrived, and I've completely abandoned the ridiculous idea of trying to write. I can barely eat; I have lost ten pounds. I manage to nap a few hours a day, but occupy most of the agonizing hours when Venus is away by exploring her house via my binoculars. Her living room has a purple, beige, and green couch, and a corduroy ottoman where she props up her feet after work. On the south wall is a framed copy of Van Gogh's *Sunflowers* hanging over a console TV. There's a deep pink chair in the corner; I can see only half an arm and cushion, also a mirrored glass stand holding a vase filled with flowers.

Upstairs: her bathroom is tiled in yellow and gray, and the shower curtain is plastic with small yellow frogs on green lily pads. A basket filled with yellow and green soaps sits on the windowsill.

It tortures me that I can't see her kitchen with my binoculars. I would consider the risk of going out again, sneaking up on her house, for the pleasure of watching her cook, and the greater pleasure of watching her eat.

Venus's bedroom, directly across from my office, is where I most like to linger. There are lace curtains in the window, always parted. The Art Deco dresser has six drawers, but the centerpiece of her room is, of course, the bed—a king-size futon, low to the floor, with a sturdy oak frame. Deep green sheets cover the mattress and a bright pink woven blanket lies folded on the end. And there are pillows—half a dozen in jewel colors. I spend hours imagining which pillow may support her left arm, her right; does she place one beneath her knees? Several would cushion her back while she reads before sleep. There's a nightstand beside the bed filled with paperback books.

What has become of George C. Simon, the professor of paleontology who was completely satisfied with his life? The confident, robust, logical, intelligent man? Did the thought occur to cross the street and knock on her door? That may have been a possibility during her first week on Lantern Hill Lane. Now I realize she is beyond my grasp. This passion has brutally enslaved my heart and mind, giving me no rest, no peace. She is the only person who can fill the emptiness, the void within me. And the moment her bronze eyes take me in, they will see only the void.

I was hopeful early on because I never saw a male visitor, but then I realized what all a man would need to be to court Venus. I have not had a "date" in five years. My only serious relationship was in graduate school. She was a sophomore, a hippie poet from Denver who delighted me with energetic bursts of devotion. I asked her to marry me and then broke the engagement after six months. She had begun to embarrass me with inappropriate displays of affection in public. She phoned at least twice a day, and she would show up at my door without warning, usually while I was working on my thesis.

Over the years, my research has proved more interesting than female companionship. I felt, before watching Venus, that women were lacking in something I couldn't quite identify. Moreover, the power of her presence has exposed the insubstantial nature of other women.

DAD NEARLY scared the life out of me. I was watching Venus move up the street, my obsession blocking out all other senses, when I heard Dad behind me. "What are you looking at? I raised you better than to be a Peeping Tom, that's a criminal offense."

I was about to lie, when he whistled. "Now there is a woman," he shouted, and nearly knocked me from my chair to get in front me. He put his gnarled hands on the screen, his face looking like a child's pressed against a candy shop window. The screen suddenly gave out and I grabbed the back of his belt just in time.

"That's a woman a man could root around in," he said as I tugged him over the sill. Then he produced a series of porcine grunts.

Terrified that she would reach her door, look up, and see me grappling with an elderly, oinking man, I quickly said, "The Tigers are playing the Blue Jays on ESPN," and Dad scrambled off to his room.

I waited for my heart to stop drumming, while the absurdity of my obsession and my inability to act on it made me swear this would stop. It had to. Then I heard guitars and maracas and I raised the binoculars. I focused on her front window and saw Venus swaying in her private, primitive dance, and my resolve dissolved like sugar on the tongue.

seven days *&* seven sins

⌇

WITH GREAT effort I write these words. The date is August 28, and the past three weeks have been as hot and dry as a desert. The water is evaporating from my tissues and blood, even the marrow of my bones. I have an image of Dad finding me in this chair, my body a mummified shell, clutching my new statuette in my right hand.

It arrived in yesterday's mail—a reproduction of the Willendorf Venus. I sent directly to the Natural History Museum of Vienna for her. The height is exactly 4⅜ inches, as is the original. The color is a subdued bronze; an artificial patina unlike the true Venus, whose oolitic limestone body was coated 24,000 years ago with ochre. How like my Venus this miniature is: the same stomach lolling over the hips, the full, soft breasts, dainty arms, thighs meeting all the way to her knees, intricate plaits of hair.

The scientific community widely considers the Willendorf Venus to be nothing more than a fertility figure, the chief arguments being the absence of facial features and of feet, and the emphasis on the labia of the vulva, which is carefully detailed and clearly visible. Therefore, they insist, she is simply a sex object.

They don't get it! She is the Earth Mother—Gaea, sprung forth from Chaos to form Earth and mated with the sky to birth the Titans. Her face is not visible because she is looking down at the earth, with a countenance of rapture that even Botticelli would have been unable to capture. You can't see her feet because they are dug into the rich Aurignacian soil.

I MISSED Venus returning from work because Dad left a pan of beans cooking on the stove that set off the smoke detector. As I tried to rush down the stairs, I twisted my ankle, and I'm sure I heard a bone snap. Hobbling into the kitchen, I went for the stepladder to shut off the alarm. Dad was under the table shouting, "Incoming, incoming, dive for the hole!"

It is now 8:30 P.M. Dad is in his room watching Thursday night Slam Down wrestling, and I am upstairs again with ice on my ankle, binoculars in one hand and my statuette in the other. Venus should return home from her weekly evening outing by 9:15, and I am ready for her. Tonight, I will do it— the last stone unturned in my descent into obsession. The street lamps come to life and the innocent laughter of children playing in the park rings through the night. On such an enchanted evening, passion sweeps away logic. I will focus my binoculars on Venus's bedroom after she has climbed the stairs, disrobed but for her gold bracelets, and reclined upon her futon to embrace the night.

Venus exits her car with a red and white cardboard bucket tucked under one arm, and I tremble with anticipation. But she doesn't go inside! She settles on her front stoop, reaches her delicate hand into the bucket and withdraws a piece of fried chicken. Her full lips open and her teeth bite gently into the drumstick. She pulls away a strip of meat, rolls her pink tongue beneath it and draws it into her mouth. She closes her dark eyes, lips glistening seductively with grease, and chews slowly. Now she swallows and my hands can barely hold the binoculars for shaking. She repeats this process ten times, and I watch, tiny white explosions of excitement at the back of my eyes, wishing that it were my hand lifting the food to her mouth.

Venus drops her chin to her chest, her spiral braids making me dizzy with desire. She laughs, and the aqueous flux of her beautiful flesh sends shocks up my spine.

As she stands and turns toward her door, this bit of stone is transformed, and my fingers caress her curves. Oh, the anticipation, oh the ecstasy! Wait! What's this . . . Oh, my God, Dad is marching across the street, and she is smiling at him.

Saturday

Saturday's Child
Works Hard for a Living

*O*PAL PALACIO gazes down at the empty Colonel Sanders bucket in her lap and weeps, remorse and self-loathing causing her 230-pound body to tremble. She closes her eyes and whispers, "God forgive me. Forgive me that the help and encouragement I got at the Pray Away Pounds meeting went in one ear and out the other as soon as I saw the KFC sign on my way home."

A large gray moth circles Opal's head and she shoos it away with a paper napkin. August has dragged on forever; even at 9:30 P.M. the temperature is 82 degrees, and it will be only a bit cooler inside the house. Her car is air-conditioned and Opal feels that contributed to her giving in because her appetite increases as the temperature drops. Even so, she had put up a fair fight. Maybe she should not have eaten the celery and carrot sticks at church, which set her stomach off rumbling for more. Opal believes it's possible that her body has developed a physical connection between her eyes and her stomach; not the simple mouthwatering most people experience when they're hungry and see food, but like a nursing mother hearing a baby cry and her breasts leaking in response. The minute Opal glimpsed the red and white KFC neon sign, her stomach growled: *Feed me, feed me now.* She would wait until she got home, then eat just one piece tonight, two for lunch tomorrow, and two for dinner. She had carried the bucket to her stoop and sat down, hoping the heat and inspiration of the star-filled sky would fill her up. After the first drumstick, her stomach said, *If you feed me more, I'll make you feel happy, and if you don't, I'll keep you up all night.*

She drops the napkin into the bucket, rises slowly, and reaches for the doorknob. A sound of staccatolike footsteps makes her turn back toward the street. An old white man is marching across Lantern Hill Lane naked as a jaybird, wearing army boots and a helmet. He is bent slightly at the waist, his arms forward and curled inward, his puckered wattle bobbing.

Opal stands frozen, clutching the bucket. The old man yells, "Praise the Lord and slam her down." He rushes Opal's stoop with surprising speed, then catches his boot on the step. His helmet rattles on the concrete as he falls into the two wide cushions of Opal's dimpled knees. His head slides down to rest on her feet. Opal feels his breath whooshing through her sandals.

"I . . . I . . . am . . . so sorry." Opal looks up to see a haggard, middle-aged man throw a blanket over the naked old man. He is out of breath and does not look at Opal when he speaks. "My name is George Simon, I live across the street. My father, Walter Simon, is sometimes . . . confused. He rarely leaves the house. I promise it won't happen again."

George pulls his father up. Walter shrugs out of his son's

grip and snatches his helmet from the porch. He oinks twice and Opal slides the bucket behind her back. She forces her most accommodating smile. "I understand. No harm done."

"Thanks, thank you. I'll take him home now," George stammers, and limps away, leading his father down Opal's front walk.

"Nice meeting you. My name is Opal Palacio," she calls after them.

OPAL SITS on the couch and props her feet on a corduroy ottoman. She had been standing all day at the bank before going to the Pray Away Pounds meeting and then was hit in the knees by a naked old man. "First neighbor I've met; too bad he didn't get to me sooner. I'd have given him that chicken he was after, instead of stuffing it in my face," she mutters.

Opal is positive that none of her neighbors have introduced themselves because she is fat. She imagines them peering from their windows with the same look of smug disgust she sees daily at the bank. It would be a relief to disappear, not to be such a visible target for ridicule every single day. Not to feel people are watching her when she eats.

That old man must have been looking at me from his window, she thinks. That's why I've had a spooky feeling of being watched whenever I'm outside. The son said he rarely leaves the house, poor old crazy thing.

Noticing a purple vein on her ankle, Opal flips down the hem of her dress. At age twenty-seven, she is too young to have varicose veins. In her nightly prayers she will include the disappearance of the vein along with the eighty pounds she wants to lose.

Opal stares at the Van Gogh *Sunflowers* poster above her TV, and her eyes glaze as they do when she becomes lost in thought. *How many pounds to go before I fit into the chair?*

OPAL'S CURRENT dilemma began last May when Suzanne Granger, the bank manager, issued a memo informing employees that one of the two Assistant Managers was leaving in September. Opal submitted an application the next day. She figured only two other employees were qualified to apply: Nadine, who had been a teller for two years, and Vincent James, her best friend, who was staying at the bank only until he had enough money saved to "blow this Popsicle stand and move to the City of Angels."

Opal Palacio had worked at Michigan Federal Bank for seven years, watching her savings grow and dreaming of a home, a roomy old house with a lawn and a garden. She was sick of tiny apartments, hauling clothes to the Laundromat, noisy tenants, and rude custodians. With an Assistant Manager's salary she could become a homeowner. Then her mother, who secretly thought she was fat, lazy, and would never amount to anything, could brag to her friends.

So confident was Opal of getting the job that she began looking for her dream house, and found it on Lantern Hill Lane within a week. At the signing, she was vaguely aware that she was creating a high-risk situation in which she might fail miserably. She had done the same thing as a child by accepting bets from her father to lose weight. For every ten dollars she earned, she ended up paying him back fifteen. In high school she bought a prom dress two sizes too small, then stayed home the night of the big dance and ordered two Supremes from Little Caesar's. Every time she had a crush on a guy, Opal told herself she'd call him after she lost ten pounds, then gain an additional five pounds from anxiety. But this was different; this was her dream house, and Opal had picked up the pen and signed the mortgage without hesitation.

The following morning Suzanne, wearing her cat-ready-to-pounce look, called Opal to her desk. With five minutes before opening, the tellers were stationed at their windows. Suzanne stood, holding Opal's application between her manicured nails. "Step over to Mrs. Reed's desk," she said.

Mrs. Reed was the Assistant Manager who would be leaving, and Opal couldn't believe her good luck—Suzanne was going to make the announcement now. Suzanne said, "The decision for our new Assistant Manager won't be made until September. However, we both know who is the most likely candidate, don't we, Opal?"

Opal had bobbed her head; she was leery of Suzanne and a bit scared of her, as every employee was. However, Opal knew something about Suzanne the others did not. Suzanne Granger, a skinny, assless woman with lacquered brown hair, had been hired as a teller a year after Opal. Suzanne was courteous to customers, willing to work late, and quick with ideas to improve marketing, which Opal had consistently done, but Mr. Peckham didn't seem to notice. Within two years Suzanne was promoted to Assistant Manager, a fact that might have stuck in Opal's throat if she had not walked into Mr. Peckham's office to find the manager's hand down Suzanne's blouse. When Peckham retired shortly thereafter, Suzanne was named bank manager. Opal had thought that Suzanne might promote her, if only to keep the potential scandal quiet.

Suzanne asked Mrs. Reed to stand, and she pulled the chair away from the desk. In all the years Opal had worked at Michigan Federal, she never gave a second glance to old Mrs. Reed's chair, but at that moment she looked at the armed, caned-seat chair and a sickening feeling spread through her. Suzanne's pale blue eyes narrowed and she lowered her voice. "This chair is identical to my chair and the other Assistant Manager's chair. They have been features of this bank for years, and we wouldn't want to break with tradition. The new Assistant Manager will need to *fit* in this chair."

Opal suddenly understood that Suzanne's method of keeping her secret was to get rid of her.

HOW MANY pounds to go before I fit in the chair? she wonders again. With the help of Pray Away Pounds, Opal has lost twenty pounds since that day last May. She pictures the chair and doubts her loss is enough. The thought makes Opal's head throb and she goes to the kitchen for a glass of lemonade.

Her Pray Away Pounds commitment requires following a nutritionally sound food plan, twenty to forty minutes of exercise five days a week, along with twenty minutes of prayer per day. Opal estimates that walking to and from work fulfills a half hour of her exercise commitment.

The prayer commitment has proved harder to fulfill.

Opal's skepticism began in Sunday school when she was five years old. The teacher had placed Noah's ark on a Velcro board and added the animals, two by two. When she put an elephant in the ark, one of the kids said, "There goes Opal." The other children snickered, and the teacher said, "That is not the way good Christians talk." But Opal didn't miss the teacher's smirk.

The litany of fat jokes increased with her age, and as an adult Opal's faith whittled down to a simple maxim: hard work earns money, money buys what I need. She began working as a baby-sitter at age twelve, she worked weekends and two nights a week at McDonald's, and she got up at 5:30 to deliver newspapers.

If she worked that hard to earn money, she could work just as hard at losing weight. At Opal's first meeting the Pray Away Pounds leader said: "You will lose pounds and inches and gain the wisdom and joy of understanding God's love in a new and vital way."

At this point, the only thing Opal understands for certain is that if she doesn't fit into the chair by the announcement date, she won't get the job, and if she doesn't get the job, she can't meet the house payments. She pours the lemonade from a frosty pitcher and goes back to the living room. She considers exercising for ten minutes, but the KFC has left her satisfied and drowsy. Besides, her favorite program will be on in a few minutes, the one starring lovely Camryn Manheim, Opal's idol since holding her Emmy award high and saying, "This is for all the fat girls."

OPAL'S FEET twitch on her king-size futon. She's dreaming about the bee girl from the MTV video, only the chubby, dancing girl has Opal's face, and as she dances down the street, there are no people, only chairs, tiny chairs that leap away on their delicate legs. By the time Opal has reached the video's dream gate, she has grown to her adult size and she's dressed in a hot pink and turquoise butterfly costume. She peers through the gate and sees a hill dotted with huge chairs. Dozens of fat people flutter down from the sky like obese angels floating, light as milkweed, to land upon their giant golden thrones. Opal pushes the gate open; there is one vacant chair, and a mouse-sized Suzanne Granger perches on the edge. Opal spreads her wings and flies toward the chair.

OPAL TAKES her time selecting an outfit for work this Friday morning. A memo may be waiting at the bank, and she wants to look her best, just in case she is asked to sit in the chair. Her clothes hang in her closet, organized into three groups: thinner, average, and extra fat. She looks with longing at the hot pink muslin outfit in the thinner group. It's the only piece of clothing that is not a dark blue or gray or black. Opal fans through the average group and chooses a black dress with gray pinstripes, which will not only make her look thinner but taller as well.

She learned fashion tips from her mother, who was not being needlessly cruel when she would say to young Opal in a dressing room, "You're too fat to wear that frilly getup. Try this one on and you'll look beautiful." She is grateful for her mother's honesty, for learning at an early age how not to draw attention to her weight.

Opal looks in her mirror and applies *Fig Stain* to her lips. She wears small gold hoops in her ears, a gold cross around her neck, and a gold bracelet on each wrist. She believes her single asset is her unusual coloring. Her hair, almond-shaped eyes, and flawless skin are all the same shade of honey bronze, and these touches of gold subtly enhance her color. She touches the cross and says, "Lord, I know I'm a backslider undeserving of your divine hand in helping me to pray away pounds, but I will eat sensibly from this day on if you will intervene on my behalf for the Assistant Manager position."

OPAL GOES directly to her workstation and reads the Friday memo. Relief immediately replaces her disappointment that the announcement will not be made until next Friday. In a week, anything could happen; God might zap fifty pounds off by next Friday. The only announcement that will be made today is August's winner for most sales. Enthusiasm among the tellers is not high because Suzanne's prize is always some cheesy gift from the dollar store. Opal has won a plastic mirror and a rubber brush.

She folds the memo in half and drops it into her wastebasket. Opal's work area is the cleanest of the six teller stations; she is the first to arrive in the morning and the last to leave at closing. This is not because she loves her job; rather, she feels a need to prove that her weight does not influence her ability to perform just as well, if not better, than the others do.

Opal hears Vincent James's voice ring out, "Good morning, Ms. Granger." Opal shakes her head and looks up to see Vincent pass Suzanne's desk, purse his lips at Opal and mouth *meow*. She loves Vincent, he's the best friend she has ever had, and he has told her that if he wasn't gay, he'd marry her in a New York minute. He's also the most beautiful man she has ever known; walking toward her, she thinks he could have stepped out of *GQ*. He stops briefly to take in the sign featuring a special rate on CDs that's propped next to the velvet ropes of the waiting line.

Once settled behind his window, Vincent leans over to Opal. "Damn, special of the day up there like a turkey on rye. Are we a bank or a deli?"

"Shhh," Opal laughs. "She's coming over here."

"Yeah, I hear the heels of those cheap shoes clicking. Tell me, why does a woman buy expensive suits and put plastic shit on her feet? I'm checking out those fly shoes of yours, ostrich?" He turns a dazzling smile to Suzanne. "Ms. Granger, have you got a present for me behind your back?"

Suzanne cuts a sharp glare at Vincent. "No, Mr. James, Opal has made the most sales for August and she gets the prize." Suzanne brings her hand from behind her back and slides a foot-long chocolate bar under Opal's window. Suzanne smirks and clicks back to her desk.

"Put that thing away, makes my pearly whites ache just looking at it," Vincent says.

Opal stares at the chocolate; despite realizing Suzanne's cruelty, her stomach rumbles, *Give me the chocolate, give it to me now.*

"I see Ms. Stranger than Strange hasn't announced the job yet. If you don't get it, sue for racial discrimination. Opal—Opal, are you listening? You've got that heifer gaze going. What's up with my girl?"

Opal faces Vincent and longs to stroke his cheek. He's the shade of black her great-grandmother calls jet-blue. "If I don't get the job, it won't be because my father is Hispanic/African-American and my mother is white. It will be because I'm too fat."

"What do you mean, too fat? Is somebody giving you a hard time? You are holding out on me, *munequita*. TGIF tonight at Flamingos and we are going to talk."

OPAL HAD skipped lunch, so by the time she arrives at the club, her stomach is screaming. Vincent waves her over to a circular table with two four-legged stools. Flamingos is known as a gay club and also known for its great music mix, which is one reason Opal frequents the place with Vincent. Another reason is that she loves to dance, and here she can actually enjoy the Pray Away Pounds exercise commitment.

"An icy margarita for you, my girl." Vincent is wearing his bright green contact lenses tonight and a slash of gold glitter under each eye. "Now you sit down and drink up and tell me what's with this too fat business. I know you've lost weight—not that you need to, 'cause you are one fine, sweet woman."

Opal lifts the drink to her lips; the salt crossing her tongue makes her stomach growl: *pizza, barbecue wings, nachos.* She empties the glass then tells Vincent the only reason she financed her house was that she was sure of getting the job, and how the next day, Suzanne pulled her nasty deal with the chair. Vincent hugs her as she continues, crying out her story about joining Pray Away Pounds, and how even with God's help she isn't going to fit her fat ass into that chair by next Friday.

"Good Lord, Opal, you don't need to put up with Ms. Stranger's shit. Ours is not the only bank in town; somebody else will snap you up if you put your résumé out there. Better yet, come with me to L.A." Vincent grins, flags down a waiter, and places an order for nachos supreme.

"Pardon me," a voice says over Cher's "Do You Believe in Love." Opal and Vincent turn to the sandy-haired young man standing at their table. "I think we're neighbors. Do you live on Lantern Hill Lane?"

"Yes, I do," Opal answers.

The man extends his hand. "I'm Hank Campbell. I live in the blue house next to yours."

Opal shakes his hand. "Pleased to meet you. I'm Opal Palacio and this is my friend, Vincent James."

Hank nods at Vincent and puts his hand in his pocket. "I've seen you walking in the neighborhood lately."

"I love this song," Vincent says. "Dance?"

Opal watches Vincent and Hank walk to the dance floor, their heads bent together to talk over the music. She watches them dance, spin, toss their heads, wave their arms high among the flock of other dancers, a glitter ball casting flashes of light swirling down on them like a snowstorm. Opal continues to watch through seven songs, she watches until the plate of nachos is bare, then slides off the stool and heads for home.

THE PRAY Away Pounds group leader opens the meeting by asking if anyone would care to testify. One woman says, "My daily scripture readings have helped me grow in the Lord and to face problems I tried to eat away."

Another woman says she has lost fifty pounds and rejoices because she no longer needs insulin injections.

A man says, "Years of dieting had only strengthened my chains of slavery to food. Now I've learned how to transfer the urge for a pie to that of hungering for God's word. Food will not fill a hungry heart, but God's love will."

Opal listens to the group's "Amens," wondering why she bothered coming. Tomorrow is Friday, the day Suzanne will pull out the chair to determine whether or not she will be promoted. And Opal has not stuck to the Pray Away Pounds nutritionally sound diet during the past week. There is no way short of a miracle she will fit into that chair tomorrow. She raises her hand and the group falls silent. Opal has never offered testimony at group.

"I want to thank you for your support and to tell you I won't be coming to the meetings anymore. I joined because in order for me to be promoted at the bank where I work, the manager said I must fit in the Assistant Manager's chair; it's a narrow, cane-seat chair with arms."

Opal notices the sneer of empathy on the face of a woman larger than Opal. She hears a disgusted grunt from the back of the room.

"I've lost at least twenty pounds since I joined, but I know that's not enough. I'm quite sure the promotion will be made tomorrow, and the manager will ask me to sit in the chair before she makes the announcement. I financed my first home last May, and without the raise in salary, I won't be able to meet the payments. Maybe I didn't pray enough; I shouldn't be here." Opal drops her head and picks up her purse.

"Ecclesiasticus 6:14," the group leader says loudly enough to make Opal lift her chin. " 'A faithful friend is a strong defense, and he that hath found such a one hath found a treasure.' Opal, you have friends here who can help."

OPAL PALACIO enters the Michigan Federal Bank at 9:05. She's wearing a lemon-yellow dress, red leather shoes, and a matching purse. Suzanne's Granger's eyes dart up, and her face remains unlined though her voice sounds as if she's on the edge of exploding. "You're late, Opal."

"There's a first time for everything," Opal says as she walks straight past Suzanne's desk.

"Stop!"

Opal stops and takes in the apprehensive expressions of the other tellers and Vincent's flashy grin.

"Before you go to your window, I want you to step over to Mrs. Reed's desk," Suzanne says.

Mrs. Reed rises, takes her purse from a drawer and her sweater from the back of the chair. "I refuse to allow you to ruin my last day of work. You should be ashamed, Suzanne Granger. Shame on you," Mrs. Reed says, wagging her finger at Suzanne, and exits the bank.

Suzanne, her lips a tight red line, yanks on Mrs. Reed's chair and turns to Opal. Opal widens her eyes. "What is it you want, Ms. Granger?"

"You know very well what I want, Opal. I want you to sit in this chair."

"But Ms. Granger, there are customers in line. I need to get to my window. Why do you want me to sit in that chair?"

Opal sees pink flushes bloom on Suzanne's cheeks.

"Because the only way you're going to get promoted is if you can fit your fat fanny in that chair, and if you can't, you are so out of here."

The bank has fallen silent. Every teller and every customer is looking at Suzanne.

"I think *you* better sit in that chair, Suzanne," Opal says, and withdraws a tape recorder from her purse. "Ever heard of Michigan's Elliot-Larsen Civil Rights Act?"

Two large people break from the back of the line and join Opal. Opal says, "I'd like to introduce my friends, Laura Kingsly, attorney at law, and Tom Feathers, south branch manager of First Capital Bank, where I'll be starting as Assistant Manager on Monday."

Laura presents Suzanne with an envelope, and Opal says, "Consider yourself served, and you're right, I am *so* out of here."

"DO YOU know why it's called a harvest moon?"

"Because it comes in autumn?" Opal answers.

"My brain's on target tonight so I'll tell you why. My son, the professor, will tell you it's called harvest moon because it shines during the autumnal equinox," Walter Simon says. "But I learned in WW2 that it's called harvest moon because it shines so bright in northern Europe that farmers can work until late at night to bring in the harvest."

"Is that a fact? Care for a second piece of apple pie, Walter?"

"No, thank you. I've got to get home and change into my uniform—WWF night. Do you ever watch wrestling, Opal?"

"I told you before, I can't watch that stuff."

"It's nice sitting with you on your stoop. You're a good cook. My wife was a good cook. Do you like your job?"

"Yes, very much."

"I'll bet you're a hard worker. You don't have to, though. You could marry me and move into my house. I've got lots of money in the bank."

"'Night, Walter," Opal says, and pats his cheek. She watches him march across Lantern Hill Lane. She stands and reaches for the doorknob, then turns toward the street, looks up to the left second story window, waves and shouts, "Good night to you too, George."

Gluttony

The Sixth Sin
Gluttony

Menu for Thanksgiving

Savory short bread
Wild mushroom soup with white truffles
Maple-syrup-glazed roast turkey with Riesling gravy
Cornbread-sourdough stuffing
Chunky apple-cranberry sauce
Baked sweet potatoes and pecans
Caramelized chestnuts and brussels sprouts
Green market apple pie
Pumpkin cake with brown butter icing
Pomegranate and apple-cider sorbet
Chocolate black-pepper icebox cookies

TOMORROW WILL be the best Thanksgiving he has had, and his first since moving in with Scott. He will dazzle their company with the fabulous dinner he's prepared. Everything is going to be perfect, from the place cards to the freshly ground hazelnut coffee. His only concern at the moment is planning how he can get away from the table when he needs to purge.

Hank Campbell has been cooking all day. He checks the list of ingredients for the pumpkin cake recipe in his November issue of *Martha Stewart Living*. He has everything he needs for a second cake except a stick of unsalted butter, so he'll make a quick trip to Mike's Market.

The first cake took thirty minutes to prepare, fifty-five minutes to bake, and was cool enough in ten minutes for Hank to eat in less than five minutes, which was approximately the same amount of time he spent jamming two fingers down his throat and purging the cake into the toilet.

He slips on his leather jacket and checks his reflection in the vestibule mirror. The purging high has worn off, and he sees his face transform, the ravenous pores opening, turning deep red and expanding until his true self is revealed: Hank the Sponge. He takes a stick of pancake makeup from his pocket and covers the broken blood vessels caused by seven years of being bulimic.

TWELVE-YEAR-OLD Angela Mayfair walks into the kitchen and drops her book bag on the table. After preparing the green market pie, Hank had just enough dough and filling left over to make a mini pie with Angela in mind. He takes the small pie from the back of the range and transfers it to a blue plate. Angela takes a bite and rolls her eyes with pleasure.

Hank returns to the sink and begins washing a pound of cranberries. He is nervous around Angela, in spite of his fondness for her. She is a constant reminder that his lover was once with a woman, however briefly, and that union produced a child. In addition, he believes Angela can see Hank the Sponge; kids often have a sixth sense regarding weaknesses.

"Thank you very much," Angela says. "I've grown two inches and gained five pounds since you've lived here."

Hank shakes the cranberry-filled sieve and hears the cells of his body squish with the movement. As soon as she goes upstairs, he'll get on the scales.

"Where did you learn to cook?"

"From books; it's easy if you follow directions." As he places sugar, wine, and chopped onion in a saucepan, Hank thinks about Grandma Campbell's kitchen in Tarpon Springs, sponge capital of the world. She lived in a pale yellow Victorian house six blocks from Hank's parents. Her kitchen was Hank's favorite place to be. His memory calls up the scents of her asparagus and peanut casserole and her famous lemon pies. *It's good to see a growing boy eat.* A week after she died, Hank's parents sold the house to a resort rental company, which turned it into a bed and breakfast.

Angela rinses her dish in the sink and glances at Hank's menu lying on the counter. "That's a lot of food for eight people, there will be eight of us, right?" She holds her fingers in the air. "You, Dad, and me; Grandma and Grandpa Mayfield, Nana Mayfield, Aunt Penny and Uncle Russ."

"That's eight," Hank says, stirring cranberries into the boiling sauce, wondering what came over him when he had offered to make Thanksgiving dinner for eight people. Angela has a knack for saying things that set him on edge, touch his insecurities. He can barely hold on to the spoon; saltwater begins seeping from his fingers.

"Did you invite your parents?" Angela asks, staring up at Hank. He won't turn away from the stove to look at her.

"They live in Florida; they always go to my brother's for holidays." Hank adds diced apples, orange zest, and ginger to the sauce.

"Is he in Florida too?"

"Yes." Hank steps back to the sink and runs the garbage disposal. He does not want to discuss his family. None of them know he is gay; at least, Hank believes they don't know. His memories of the last Thanksgiving spent in Tarpon Springs are ones he would rather forget. Dad strutted around in shorts, 140 pounds of bones, veins, and flesh, never sitting down to eat but heaping food on everyone else's plates, then tsk-tsking, "Calories, calories," when anyone asked for seconds. Mother picked at her food, still a size six despite her craving for sweets; she had kept herself thin by eating only sweets. She had told Hank that she was afraid Dad would leave her if she gained weight, and Hank believed he would have too. His older brother, tall and muscular, was oblivious to everything but the food in front of him. His favorite expression was, "You can eat like a horse if you shit like an elephant." Fat was the worst thing that could happen in Hank's family, anything soft and round was the object of horrified disgust and ridicule. Hank was determined not to bring a trace of the pudgy Florida boy into Scott Mayfield's house on Lantern Hill Lane.

Angela tugs on Hank's shirttail. "Do you think you could take Dad and me to Florida sometime? I've never been there."

Suddenly, Hank is ravenous. He needs to eat now, and eat a lot. "Angela, I have to give a four o'clock lesson at the pool. Your dad called earlier and said he would be home by four." He runs a finger back and forth over the callused knuckles of his right hand. Angela watches this nervous gesture she has seen many times before.

"Go ahead, I'll be fine."

HANK POPS the glove compartment of his '91 Mustang and empties his cache onto the seat. Scott won't ride in it, and he wants to buy Hank a new SUV, a Wrangler or a Blazer. But Hank has a sentimental attachment to the old Mustang, the car that carried him out of Florida; his private cave stocked with food, meals on wheels. Besides, Scott has already given Hank way too much, more than Hank feels he deserves, and each gift puts him further into an emotional debt he'll never be able to repay.

Pulling out of the drive, he rips open a package of Slim Jims and eats them two at a time. The last thing he'd eaten was the pumpkin cake, and he was only able to get through the day's cooking by thinking about his glove compartment goodies. By the time he reaches Capital Sport Complex, he has consumed a snack size bag of chips, a package of corn nuts, a king-size Snickers bar, and four Twinkies.

Hank goes directly to the men's locker room and purges the contents of his stomach. He lied to Angela; the group lesson isn't until 4:45, but he had to get out of the house, away from her questions he can't answer.

Hank steps on the scales, 152 pounds, which is healthy for a five-nine, twenty-three-year old. However, he feels his life would be better if he dropped to 145. During intimate moments, Scott has said he's worried about Hank's health, that he should gain at least ten pounds. Scott doesn't know that once over 165, Hank the Sponge cannot be controlled.

Hank changes into his Speedos and warm-up suit and goes to the juice bar. Ellie has been managing the bar since Hank began working at the center last January. She has a fruit smoothie with protein powder waiting for him on the counter.

"You're early," she says.

"I want to get a few laps in before class."

"I should too, knowing how I'll pig out tomorrow. Are you and Scott and Angela having turkey?"

Hank rubs his thumb over his calluses. All the employees know about Hank and Scott's relationship. Scott is the CPA who handles finances for the complex, and their names are listed in the office directory with the same address and phone number. "Yeah, see you later," Hank says, heading for the pool.

He removes his warm-up suit and begins stretching out. There's no one else in the pool and he is grateful. Gazing across the blue water and the white-roped lanes, he can't help thinking about the Tarpon Swim Club, the years of competition, the medals and trophies he left in Florida. By age fourteen he made the Junior Nationals in freestyle and backstroke. At age sixteen he qualified for the Junior Olympics, the same year Quinn joined the club, the same year Hank began bingeing and purging.

Hank tries to avoid recalling the past; he pictures Scott's dining room table spread with roast turkey and all the trimmings, imagining the taste of each dish as it crosses his palate. He imagines how proud Scott will be, and that it's little enough to do for the man who has given him so much, for the man he loves so much it scares him.

He steps up on a diving block and Quinn's face floats to the surface. He was Hank's first love, the boy who introduced him to pleasure: Quinn behind him on the pool ladder, both of them clutching the aluminum rails; the same boy who next day poked his stomach in front of the team and called him "sponge boy."

Quinn didn't speak to him after that day, and that's when Hank's fixation on sponges began. With snorkel and fins, he collected them in the warm coastal Florida waters: yellow sponges, wool sponges, grass sponges, tube and vase sponges. He got up at dawn to watch the weekly auctions on Sponge Dock. He wrote a report for biology class, the scientific terms of which he has long forgotten.

Hank remembers the simplest yet most pertinent facts: sponges have no tissue or organs, but an aggregation of cells supporting a network of chambers and canals that connect to open pores on the surface; most sponges are hermaphroditic; sponges feed by attaching themselves to something solid, drawing water through their pores, filtering out the nutrients, and then ejecting it out through an opening. Food was solid, food was nutritious, but too much made you fat. "It's a sin to be fat," Dad said. "No one loves you if you're fat," Mom said. "Sponge boy," Quinn said.

During his teenage years, late at night, by the glow of his aquarium light, Hank would consume a package of Oreos, or a box of Goo Goo Clusters, or whatever sweet and sticky thing he could buy on his way home from school, and eject it before allowing himself to drift into a sugary sleep.

Hank dives in the pool and coasts, feeling his pores soaking up water, shifting through his chambers, propelling him forward—Hank the Sponge in his natural element.

By the time he completes his third lap, he sees the pool's bottom as a mass of sponges: red ball, orange fancy, blue tube, yellow tree, grass, and willow. He wants to expel his breath and sink down among them deep and silent, where there are no expectations of him except to feed.

⌁

SCOTT AND Angela are in the kitchen serving up the Caesar salad, rigatoni, and garlic bread Scott picked up at Antonio's.

"I heard your car," Scott says as Hank enters the kitchen. "I thought we'd eat light, considering the spread you're creating for tomorrow." Scott walks over to Hank and kisses his cheek. Hank's eyes shift to Angela, who smiles demurely before looking away.

Hank pulls out a chair and sits at the table. They have talked about this; he has told Scott he's not comfortable showing affection in Angela's presence. Scott insists it's essential for her emotional development to see the two most important adults in her life being affectionate. Yet, Hank has to practically stand on his head to get Scott's attention anyplace outside of the house. He refuses to go to Flamingos, and Hank doesn't believe Scott's excuses that the music is too loud and the crowd's too young. Hank also does not believe he is important to Angela. Moreover, if he were honest with himself, he would admit that he doesn't want to be important to Angela because he will disappoint her. He doesn't want to grow attached to her; that would make it harder on both of them when Scott eventually tires of him and asks him to leave.

"Is that all you're going to eat, Hank?" Scott asks.

"What?" Hank looks up from his plate.

"I asked if that's all you're going to eat."

"Sorry, I was thinking about the Butterball. Besides, I'm getting flabby around the middle."

"Are you serious?" Angela gazes across the table at Hank, her dark eyes wide with exaggeration. "You could be a stand-in for Leonardo DiCaprio. You're the cutest guy I know, except for Dad."

"Way to butter up the old man," Scott says. "Oh, Penelope phoned at the office today and said she's bringing a salad. Can I help you in the kitchen, Hank?"

"No, thanks. I just have to fix the sorbet, and that's a quick recipe. I think I'll go for a walk before I get started."

Scott looks at his watch. "MacNeil-Lehrer time, but I'll come with you if you like."

"Go relax; I won't be gone long."

BEFORE SETTING off on his walk, Hank reaches under the seat of the Mustang and retrieves the two Whoppers and chocolate shake he bought after class. Walking down the street, bolting the burgers, he thinks, Michigan autumns are the best. Autumn in Florida is hot, damp, and bugs the size of dough-nuts kamikaze dive into windshields. But here the air is crisp and clean; everything seems to slow, like leaves drifting off the trees. He pictures the state of Michigan as he remembers it from the road atlas he followed when he left Miami.

After graduating from high school, Hank made plans to get out of Tarpon Springs, and Miami's bright beacon of light drew him to its glittering shore. After four years of working as a lifeguard or swim instructor by day, clubbing and cruising by night, he had lost his innocence and Miami had lost its luster.

One Saturday morning, head and back aching, face puffy and gums swollen from overpurging, Hank went to a 7-Eleven for Alka Seltzer. Waiting in line, he picked up a road atlas. It was all the blue, fresh water that caught his eye, five Great Lakes and straight north on 75. Both he and Hank the Sponge could agree on Michigan.

Now, reaching the entrance to Lantern Hill Lane, Hank crosses the street and heads back toward the park. The house windows look to him like aquariums lit in a dark room, people floating back and forth behind the glass. He thinks of the aquarium he had at his parents' house and the night hours spent watching his sponges, admiring their efficiency. In those earlier years, purging was simply a way for him to relieve the pain of overeating, but somewhere along the line, it became something more, a ritual form of relieving the sadness, stress, guilt, and loneliness that grew with each passing year.

Tonight, Hank's stress level is at an all-time high. He has

not met Scott's sister and her husband or Nana Mayfield. He met Scott's parents once on a trip to their home in Grosse Pointe, and he was as nervous as a whore in church, as his Grandma Campbell would say.

Hank's pace slows; his cells are madly undulating with the effort of trying to filter beef. As he nears the park at the end of the street, his shoes fill with seawater. He sloshes over to a large white oak, inserts two fingers in his mouth and purges onto the base of the tree.

THROUGH THE east-facing window, Hank sees Scott watching Angela play chess on her computer. His hand is on Angela's shoulder and Hank can tell he's giving her advice on the next move. Hank knows she will listen, but play the game to win.

"Just like her mother," Scott has said in private more times than Hank would like. He wants to say, "Hell, you hardly knew her mother. You fucked her until she got pregnant and paid her ten grand for custody of Angela." Hank didn't believe Scott's story about not trusting artificial insemination, how some wacko doctor inseminated all his patients with his own sperm. He thinks Scott enjoyed the challenge of making love to a woman, and will probably want to do it again. But he keeps his thoughts to himself because he loves Scott and is afraid of losing him. Angela may look like her mother, but inside she has the same stubborn streak and unflagging optimism as Scott. She's so beautiful and perfect, how can Hank the Sponge compete with her? How can Scott ever love him even half as much? Hank turns from the window, gets in the Mustang, and drives north toward downtown.

THERE IS not much of a crowd at Flamingos, maybe a dozen people seated and four couples dancing to a club track. Hank orders a Rusty Nail, and the waiter brings it to the table along with a bowl of white corn chips and salsa. Hank eats one chip and all he can taste is the salt; it's not just his mouth, his entire body is watering. He empties the bowl, but his ravenous cells need more saline. He goes to the bar and asks for a bowl of pretzels and a bowl of mixed nuts. He finishes them off before the waiter returns, and he orders a second drink and a refill on the corn chips.

Hank clasps his hands behind his neck and leans back in the chair. Santana's "Smooth" begins, and the Latin beat calls up images of Miami, the painted, glittering men dancing at clubs, the hot quick moments of passion, faces and names forgotten with the rising of the sun. Hank's body expands and flows over the chair. *I don't deserve the home I have here; I don't deserve Scott—shit.* He checks his watch and slides out of the chair. *Scott will be pissed off, gotta hurry, but first . . .*

Hank falls to his knees before the commode, fingers down his throat, but Hank the Sponge does not want to relinquish the soothing sodium. He gags and tries again, this time successfully, just as he hears the outer door swing open. He scrambles to his feet and sits quietly, waiting for the sound of urine hitting water, the flush, and exit.

"Are you done? That's the only toilet in here and I have to puke too."

Hank reluctantly opens the door, and a muscular man pushes past him. In the next second, before Hank can turn away, the man shoots a stream of vomit into the commode from a standing position. Hank hurries to the sink and busies himself washing his hands. The man comes to the sink beside him and glances at the callused fingers of Hank's right hand. "I used my fingers until I got pumped up. Work out twice a day and this washboard of muscles can empty my stomach in five seconds."

Hank rubs his thumb over his callused fingers and reaches for the paper towel dispenser.

"You don't need to be embarrassed, lots of us do it." The man smiles, a dazzling white smile, and Hank guesses his teeth are capped. Hank's dentist told him if he didn't stop purging, the enamel on his front teeth would be gone to the point of needing caps within a year.

"It's the Hercules-chic thing. Used to be you could never be too rich or too thin. These days, if you look thin, you look sick, right?" The man wets his fingers and runs them through his hair. "It was the Soloflex guy that got me started. You remember that ad or are you too young?"

"Yeah, sure, I remember it," Hank says.

"All these women saying they've got it so bad, having to diet and exercise to keep thin and keep a man. Well, today's boys are obsessed with physique—you can never be too built or too built. I'm Mark," the man says, extending his hand, flexed bicep obvious below his short-sleeve shirt.

"Hank."

"Hank Campbell?"

"Yeah, how did you know?"

"A guy's out there looking for you. Tall, dark hair, suit and tie, older."

Hank rushes into the main room and sees only the faces of the men who had been there since he arrived. He tells the bartender his name is Hank Campbell and asks if someone was looking for him. The bartender says the guy just left.

⌒

"I DON'T even want to know why you felt the need to go to that club tonight, but you should be aware that cruising is dangerous—for both of us."

Here we go, Hank thinks, dumping a tray of ice into a large metal bowl. He pours a cup of cider into a saucepan, adds half a cup of sugar, and turns the heat to high.

"Not that I'm accusing you of being with someone else. However, I don't need to tell you that promiscuity has serious pitfalls."

"Scott, I wasn't with anyone. I was in the men's room when you came in and—"

Scott raises his hand. "I don't need details. You said you were going for a walk, and then I saw that your car was gone. You're free to come and go as you please, but it's only common courtesy to let me know when you change your plans."

He had been on the verge of telling Scott exactly what he was doing in the men's room. Scott would be horrified, lecture him on the health risks, and then recommend a shrink. Hank sets the pan of boiling syrup in the ice bath.

"I didn't think the gap in our ages would make that big a difference, but perhaps I was wrong. I just want to make you happy," Scott says in that smooth-as-silk voice that made the back of Hank's neck tingle when he first heard him speak.

"You're not my father, Scott. I don't love my father; I love you." Hank cuts a pomegranate in half, red juice bleeding onto his fingers. "I'm sorry I didn't tell you I was going out."

Hank pushes a pomegranate half onto the citrus press. He keeps pressing until all the juice is extracted, leaving only spongy pulp, and he feels Scott's arms close around his waist.

Upstairs in their bed, waves of passion turn the room aqueous, Scott's voice a faint rush of sound echoing in his ears. Tomorrow will be the best Thanksgiving he has had, his first with Scott. Hank hangs on tightly, hoping this man, this house, will be enough to grow on.

Avarice

The Seventh Sin
Avarice

ND REMEMBER to have your pets spayed or neutered," Bob Barker says as he steps out of Mavis Otis's black-and-white Motorola TV.

"I'm getting mighty tired of hearing you say that, Bob. It's not very gentile, and I don't know what animals have to do with *The Price Is Right.* Guess it's your pet project."

Bob chuckles, and Mavis says, "I can be funny when I want. I haven't had a pet since 1931. Patches was my pony's name. Somebody stole her one night, and I heard Papa say to Mama that horse meat was as good as hamburger to the hungry. People were desperate during the Great Depression." Mavis leans her head back on the tattered Empire couch and sighs, "I loved that pony."

Bob sits in the overstuffed chair to her right, and Mavis notices a five dollar bill sticking out from the seat cushion. Bob plucks the bill free and holds it between two black-and-white fingers.

"You think that one's too full, Bob?" Mavis gets to her feet and unzips the cushion. She reaches inside and pulls out a heap of money. "Where should I hide it?"

Mavis totters along the living room's narrow path of bare floor, past five-foot stacks of newspapers and magazines, piles of mail, broken chairs, cracked tables, broken record players, and useless televisions, into the kitchen. Bob follows, his white hair brushing cobwebs from the hall chandelier.

Mavis steps over a box of glass bottles, around a crate full of aluminum potpie tins, and opens a bread box on the counter. Finding it stuffed with cash, she tries a cookie jar, a dusty butter churn, and a rusted canister set, but all are jammed full.

"Don't start on me, Bob. Five banks say I've exceeded FDIC guarantees, and the only bank in town that doesn't have some of my money is Michigan Federal. I went there last week, and a big fat teller said she was my neighbor. You're so all fired quick with numbers, how much do you figure that fat girl spends in a week for food?" Mavis turns to find Bob perched on a wooden chair, his expression perplexed.

"I might be old, but I ain't crazy. She'd blab to everyone on the street about how much old Miss Otis has, then when that rainy day comes again, the great collapse, they'll be pounding on my door like sinners trying to hitch a ride on Noah's Ark." Mavis opens the door of a coal-burning stove and stuffs the money inside.

"That was a real nice kitchen you gave away today on the Showcase Showdown, and an all expense paid trip to Chicago to boot. Did I tell you that Papa took me to the Chicago World's Fair in '33? I was fourteen, and Papa bought me a straw hat with cherries on the brim. Don't give a hoot about going to Chicago now, but I sure could use those appliances.

How about it, Bob? How about a new kitchen for your old friend Mavis?"

Bob waves his arm expansively over the kitchen clutter, his gray suit sleeve crackling with electricity.

"I'd find space for it, always do, don't I? Are you hungry, Bob? I do believe it's lunchtime. We can have peanut butter and jam or those Oriental noodles. Noodles it is, something hot on a cold winter day."

Mavis opens a cupboard that's stocked top to bottom with Ramen noodle packages. "A case of fifty for five dollars— that'd be a good one for Bob's Bargain Bar, don't you think?"

Bob nods and flashes his Hollywood smile. Mavis rinses out one of the dirty pans piled in the sink and puts water on to boil. The doorbell rings, and Mavis looks at the one kitchen clock that still works. "That will be the mail. Must be something big he can't fit through the slot," Mavis says, and scurries back along the path to the front door. Bob has to break into a trot to keep up with her. Mavis turns and whispers, "You go hide, Bob. Not in the closets either, there's a skeleton in every one of them."

The postman holds a cardboard box and wears an irritated expression. "Miss Otis, I have asked you repeatedly to please clear your porch. It's dangerous, and during the holidays my bag is extra heavy. If I can't get freely to your door, you won't be receiving your mail."

"Okay, okay, cut the gab and give me my mail, you're letting cold air inside." The man gives her the box and removes a stack of envelopes from his bag.

"Happy holidays to you too, Miss Otis," he says, handing Mavis the envelopes.

Mavis slams the door and squints at the writing on the box. "Mavis Otis, 12 Lantern Hill Lane, Lansing, Michigan—that's me. It's from one of those banks, Bob. I can guarandamntee you it's something cheap." Mavis claws the box open and removes a round Christmas-decorated tin. "Not like in the old days when all the bankers knew Papa and would send a toaster or a radio for Christmas. I'll bet that old Crosley radio still works, probably worth two hundred bucks or so as an antique by now. Do you remember where I put it, Bob? Oh, a fruitcake, we can have some for dessert—heavens to Betsy, the noodles!"

〜

"CARE FOR another slice of fruitcake while I look over the mail? Don't mind if I do." Mavis breaks off a chunk of cake from the tin set next to her on the couch.

Bob pats his stomach, and Mavis says, "Fruitcake will sit like a stone, keep you full for hours. Now, let's see . . . electric bill—ha, only thirty-five dollars. What do you think my neighbors pay? Twice as much, minimum, and every house at least half the size of mine. Closed off every vent except for the living room, which suits me fine. This couch is more comfortable than any bed. Papa had it sent all the way from Paris, you know. If I stick my nose in the seams, I can still smell Mama's lilac talc."

Bob turns up his nose and looks to the right.

"So I don't smell of lilacs. If I had two maids and a cook like Mama did, I could float around in a tub of lilac water too. Tubs are dangerous for old ladies. Would you be willing to

208

drag my naked body out if I fell and cracked my head? Thought not," Mavis snaps, and opens another envelope.

"Hmm, a gift for you of Christmas stamps and please send a donation in the enclosed envelope."

Mavis slips the letter under the couch and shoves the stamps in her sweater pocket. "Waste not, want not, Papa always said. What? You think I should send money to these shysters? Did I ask them to send me these stamps? What percentage of the donations do you think goes to poor orphans compared to what pads the company's bank account?"

She opens another envelope and takes out a Christmas card. "Well if that don't beat all. You'll never guess who this is from." Mavis holds the card up for Bob to see, and he cocks his head inquisitively.

"The granddaughter of my worthless cousin Ned. Says she wants to come visit me because she hasn't seen me since she was a little girl. She writes, *You're the only Otis left and I'd like my kids to meet you.* Bob, I remember, clear as if it were yesterday, the last time Ned and his clan were here from Wisconsin. It was for Papa's funeral back in 1968. 'You don't need this great big house, Mavis, and all this furniture. Why, all Grandma Otis's belongings are here too. I wouldn't mind taking a few things off your hands, as keepsakes to remember Grandma and Uncle Charles,' Ned said, all the while his eyes roaming."

Bob rolls his eyes sympathetically.

"You betcha I was mad as a wet hen. I asked him who had kept Papa's records, accounts, and house in order since 1940. Who took care of Mama and then Papa when they were sick and dying? 'It sure wasn't you, Ned,' I said. Him standing there turning his hat around in his hands. Then I went upstairs to get Papa's will to show the buzzard that everything in this house was mine, and I caught his wife going through Mama's dresser. Chased the bad bunch of them out with my broom. No reason his granddaughter would be any different. Probably thinks I got one foot in the grave and wants to add up the booty. I need every cent I have. Who is going to give two hoots about an old lady when the crash comes? I'll show them all—I won't be selling apples on the street, I'll be sitting pretty."

Bob gives Mavis a wink, and she says, "You're wasting your charm on me, save it for those girls on your show. I must admit that you're a snappy dresser. Of course, you don't have to pay for those fine duds you wear on TV." Mavis detects a slight frown of disapproval on Bob's black-and-white face.

She tucks a stray lock of hair under her purple stocking cap. "Well, I know my clothes ain't brand new, but they keep me warm. Why should I waste good money on overpriced ugly clothes at the mall? I got trunks and closets full of clothes, Mama's dresses and Grandma's too. Now, let me get to this other piece of mail."

Again the doorbell rings, and Mavis huffs with exasperation as she rises from the couch. She shouts at the door, "Who is it?"

"Steve Castellani. I'm your neighbor and a police officer. Could you open your door, please."

"Okay, but you better have your badge out, and I've got a baseball bat in my hand," Mavis yells, and picks up the bat leaning against the wall. Bob chuckles from behind her, and she tells him to go hide behind the newspapers. She whispers, "If word gets out that you're living here, the whole town's going to be pestering me for your autograph."

Mavis cautiously opens the door a crack and sees a man dressed in uniform on her porch. *Better be nice, Mavis,* Bob calls from his hiding place.

"Mrs. Otis, there's been a complaint about the amount of trash on your property. It's also been reported that you have stacks of papers inside that present a fire hazard. May I come in?"

"It's *Miss* Otis, and no you may not, unless you've got a warrant, buster."

"Okay, Miss Otis. I won't write you up today if you'll promise to get your porch and yard cleared of debris. Here's a card with my name and home phone number. I can help you locate people to haul this away. Miss Otis, did you hear me?"

"Which house do you live in, sonny?"

"Number five."

"Slide that card under the storm door."

"Right. You have a Merry Christmas, Miss Otis."

"You betcha."

Mavis closes the door and sputters, "When the ocean wears rubber pants to keep its bottom dry." She returns to the couch, Bob following at her heels. "I'll bet you dollars to doughnuts that snotty mailman reported me, went right to the cop's house and tattled. Sit down, Bob. You make me nervous hovering over me, grinning like that. Oh, that's right, one more letter."

Mavis pulls a card from the envelope. "It's a Christmas greeting from Florence Lathrop; she always sends me a card. Christmas stinks, Bob, everyone rushing around to spend, spend, spend, going into debt to outdo last year's gifts. And the girls on your show look stupid in those red velvet skimpy dresses. Now don't pout, Bob. Did I ever tell you about Florence and me?"

Bob sets his elbows on his thighs and leans forward in the chair.

"I met Florence my first year at college; we were both studying mathematics. I was supposed to attend Bryn Mawr, the college that graduated Mama, but because of the Great Depression, Papa said he couldn't afford it, so I lived at home and studied at Michigan Agricultural College. He bought me a 1937 Packard to drive to classes, and oh brother, the fun Florence and I had with that car. My second year Mama had her first stroke and I had to drop out to take care of her. Florence graduated—she was a professor at some college in California before she retired. She was the best friend I ever had and the only one still living. It was Florence who introduced me to Timothy."

Mavis picks up the card from her nephew's granddaughter and carefully tears it along the seam. "I'll use this half as a post-card to send to Florence. It's cold today, isn't it, Bob? I could use another layer of clothes."

Mavis snaps her fingers, "I've got it," and she is up from the couch, hustling toward the staircase. She cautiously places her feet on the few spaces clear of clutter: a jug filled with pennies, stacks of mildewed books, a dented bugle, and an old hair dryer litter the first three steps. Halfway up, she turns to see Bob standing at the bottom shaking his head.

"Come on, you sissy. Pretend this is your Cliff Hanger game with the mountain climber. Don't expect me to yodel, and I'd prefer it if you didn't either."

Bob crosses his arms and looks with disdain at the clutter around his feet.

"You want me to throw everything out, do you? Well, let

me tell you, Mr. Price Is Right, what led to Mama's stroke. One day before Papa went to work he dropped the newspaper over his mail. Later, Mama saw the paper lying on the dining table and she scooped it up and threw it in the trash. The ten thousand dollar money order to Papa went out with the paper, and by the time Papa called the bank to find out when they were sending his money, somebody had cashed the order, some trash-picking thief!" Mavis screeches, and keeps climbing all the way to the third floor. She is looking out the gabled attic window when Bob enters the room and sits on one of a dozen trunks.

"During the Great Depression lots of people lost their homes and jobs. Papa had worked hard to get where he was, and because of that lost money order, he had to sell most of his property in order to keep this house and pay his employees. When I was a little girl, this was the only house for miles around. Papa owned acres and acres of land, all the way to the river. That park was mine; it's where I rode my pony, and there was a gazebo where I had tea parties in the summer. In winter, Papa had his workmen flood it so I could ice skate. I wore a white fur coat and a muff to match, and Papa wore . . . That's why I came up here."

She goes from one trunk to another, digging through until she pulls a raccoon coat from a large leather-bound trunk. "Papa's coat!" Mavis slips into the coat and walks to a full-length mirror propped in a corner. The coat drags behind her, clearing a path on the dusty floor. She looks at her image and cackles, "Look at that funny old shriveled-up face poking out."

Bob appears behind Mavis's reflection and he is scowling fiercely.

"I know all about your fur flap protests, Bob—that's all it

is to me, a bunch of flap. These raccoons have been dead over fifty years. This was Papa's favorite coat, and it's so warm. Well, I don't care to have you frowning at me all afternoon, so why don't you just go downstairs and get back into that TV."

Mavis paws around in the trunks for ten minutes, waiting until she is sure Bob is good and gone. She stops when her hand touches something small, cool, and metal. She stares at the heart-shaped silver locket for a long while before slipping it around her neck and walking down the stairs for an afternoon nap.

"HEAVENS TO Betsy, can't a body get any rest in this neighborhood?" Mavis draws the raccoon coat tightly about her and walks along the path to the front door. "Bob, get away from there. I ain't answering—could be that cop again."

Bob steps to the side and looks out the glass panel beside the door.

"It's a boy, you say? What kind of uniform?" Mavis opens the door a crack. "What do want, kid?"

"My name is Jacob Delaney and I'm collecting newspapers for Cub Scout pack 603's paper drive. Officer Delaney said you had a lot of newspapers on your porch, and you sure do. I'll be glad to take them away."

Mavis pokes her head out the door. "And I suppose you want to come inside for papers too so you can case the joint, then bring back some of your friends at night and rob me blind."

Bob clears his throat and says, *Be gentle, Mavis. The boy's father died last year.*

"Mine's dead too!" Mavis snaps, and Jacob's eyes widen with fear. He begins scrambling down the front steps and trips over an old washtub. *If he's hurt, his mother can sue you, Mavis,* Bob murmurs.

"He's okay. Look, he's already going down the sidewalk."

If you don't clear off the porch, you'll have to pay a fine on top of paying a rubbish company to haul it away. Jacob's price is right.

"Wait—kid, you can take the newspapers on the porch. But if you come across any money, remember it belongs to me, and Santa won't be good to a boy who steals from an old lady."

Mavis shuts the door and sputters her way back to the couch, "Neighborhood's going to hell in a handbasket. What happened? When did I get so old?" Mavis's hand wanders to her throat and closes around the locket.

What have you got there, Mavis?

"On our first date we went to the Strand to see *The Wizard of Oz,* summer of 1939. When I drove him home in the Packard, he said he'd like to take me over the rainbow. Timothy didn't have a car, didn't have much of anything other than good looks, charm, and a head full of dreams. I told you Florence introduced us. He worked at the dairy store on campus, and Florence was in there nearly every day for ice cream. Timothy and I dated that summer, then Mama had her stroke in the fall and I had to leave school. When I was with Timothy, I didn't feel so sad about all I was missing. Papa didn't like him one bit."

Bob's forehead creases with concerned interest, and for an instant he fades out, then reappears in the chair.

"He said Timothy was a fortune-hunter out to marry into money. I didn't believe him, but Papa was right—Papa was always right."

Mavis curls up on the couch and pulls her feet under the coat. "Timothy and I made plans to elope on the Sunday before Christmas. Papa got wind of it; I don't know how, but he had spies everywhere. Come that Sunday, I sat in my room, wearing a beige lace dress, my suitcase packed, watching the clock, waiting for midnight to slip out and pick up Timothy. Five minutes before twelve, Papa came into my room and handed me a note. I recognized Timothy's handwriting. He'd written, *By the time you read this I'll be on a train headed west. You know how I've dreamed of going to the golden city by the bay. With the five hundred dollars your father gave me, I'll be set for a year. Sorry kiddo.*"

Mavis pulls the locket outside of her coat and opens the silver casing. "He broke my heart, Bob. That's Timothy on the right and me on the left."

Mavis looks up and sees horizontal lines running through Bob's suit. "I thought this locket was lost that year; it went missing from my jewelry box. I found it this afternoon in one of Papa's trunks. Timothy broke my heart, but it was Papa who locked it away, wasn't it, Bob? Bob?"

The chair is empty, and Mavis's eyes dart around the living room. She walks to the kitchen and calls for Bob again. At the bottom of the staircase she yells, "I'm too old for games, Bob. Come on down."

A creaking noise comes from the front hall, and Mavis hurries toward the sound. The door is closed tightly with the lock in place. She steps into a pair of rubber galoshes, slides the lock and opens the door. Mavis can see clearly to the street; not only are the stacks of newspapers gone from her porch, but all the trash as well. And Mavis hears a song, sung cherubim-sweet.

It's a Christmas carol Mavis has not heard since she was a child.

The singer is a young girl dressed in a red snowsuit shoveling Mavis's sidewalk. Mavis opens her mouth to speak, but the song makes her pause and try to recall the German lyric her grandmother sang. The effort makes her irritable.

"Little girl, you, redhead. What are you doing on my sidewalk?" Mavis says.

The girl straightens and looks up at the porch. "Shoveling snow," she says.

"Why?"

"When I finished our sidewalk, I saw this was the only place on the block that wasn't shoveled. It upset my sense of aesthetics. I like your coat, it's really cool."

"What's your name?"

"Angela Mayfair."

"I can't pay you."

"I wasn't expecting to be paid."

"You won't go far with that attitude, miss. Have you seen Bob Barker out there?"

"Nope, but I love *The Price Is Right*. I've watched it every day of Christmas vacation."

"Angela Mayfair, do you like fruitcake?"

Sunday

Sunday's Child

Born on the Sabbath Day
Is fair and wise and good and gay

MY NAME is Angela Mayfair. I am twelve years old and I live at 10 Lantern Hill Lane in Lansing, Michigan. I have lived on this street all my life and I know everything about this neighborhood. Mavis Otis said the neighborhood is going to hell in a handbasket. I asked her what she meant, but Mavis didn't answer me. When Dad came home, I asked him, and he didn't know, but he said I should try the Internet.

All I could find out, and I'm very good at finding things on the 'net, was that the expression was recorded as early as 1629. The web page writer assumed that the word *handbasket* suggests something easily and speedily done.

That's not correct. A long time ago, ladies probably carried baskets instead of purses and they would decorate them with ribbons and flowers. I believe going to hell in a handbasket means something is going bad, but looking pretty on the way.

Mavis also told me not to open any closets because there were skeletons in all of them. You might have laughed, thinking Mavis was making a joke. I did not laugh; I knew she wasn't joking.

I know this and more because I am a Millennium Extrasensory Evolution Kid. There are kids like me in neighborhoods throughout America. We know how to recognize each other. We use words carefully, know what to reveal and what to keep secret. We hear the words you meant to say. We are patient and mild.

What Mavis Otis meant to say is that the neighborhood looks pretty on the outside but is going bad inside. What's inside? People. Mavis doesn't know anyone on Lantern Hill Lane. Well, she said a cop and a boy had been there earlier, but she couldn't remember their names. If she doesn't know anyone on Lantern Hill Lane, how can she say the neighborhood is going to hell in a handbasket?

I know what you're thinking, and you are wrong. You think an old lady with nothing to do but hide her money would watch the neighborhood, would want to see what her neighbors look like and what is going on every minute. You think she is prejudiced against people of color, that she views homosexuality as a sin, that she thinks teenagers are wild and mean, that fat people are lazy, cops are corrupt, and short people are to be feared.

We have been taught to be afraid. Don't talk to strangers, don't pet stray animals, never walk home alone. Children are beaten, raped, and murdered by adults and by other children. Predators lurk around schools and parks to get you into their cars or hooked on drugs. Predators lurk in cyberspace. There are pesticides in food and pollution in the atmosphere. We are taught to trust no one. Teachers teach us not to trust our parents, and parents teach us not to trust our teachers.

What Mavis meant to say is that nobody on this street cares enough to get to know her because they are afraid. The better you get to know a thing, the less fearful it becomes, and without fear, trust can grow, and trust builds familiarity, and then skeletons dance out of their closets.

Mavis doesn't watch the neighborhood, but I do. The first thing you drew in school was your house, I know I'm right about this. Maybe your mother's smiling head was in the window, a fat dog on your lawn. As a kid, your house was your whole world, and as an adult your home's brick or wood stands between you and the world. As a Millennium Extrasensory Evolution Kid, I can see through walls. You don't believe me. Walk with me down the street and I'll show you.

The first house is where the Timmicks live. Arnie Timmick is a dwarf and Faye Timmick is beautiful. Their skeleton is in the basement pantry, a huge shadow that only comes out in the spring and the rest of the time squats black and ugly in Mrs. Timmick's head.

Across the street are the Delaneys. No skeleton, but there is a ghost that can't leave until Megan and Jake are whole and happy, and that will be very soon.

Next to them is Mrs. Blanchard. A year ago she found Mr. Blanchard dead in the snow under her window, a smile frozen on his face. Calvin doesn't haunt the house, but Harriet has a skeleton in her neat and tidy den, a guilty skeleton.

Across the street at number 3 are Mr. and Mrs. Cavendish, Cora and Bill, the orchid couple. The baby she's expecting in

May is one of us, one of the Millennium Extrasensory Evolution Kids. Number 5 is where the Castellanis live. Gloria tries to lock up her skeleton by working hard at Amelio's restaurant, but at night the memories of what might have been wrap around her like a shroud.

Number 6 is where Grace Van Houghton lives. She stood up to her skeleton last spring and drove it out of her house. Over there in number 7, Alex and Jane Williams are talking about her brother. She's worried because she hasn't heard from him in months. Jane's skeleton is imagination of her brother's nightmares of bombs and bloody hands reaching to pull him farther away from her.

The Lovejoys live in number 9. Rebecca will deny the fact that there's a skeleton in her closet. Most of the time she's either too busy or too consumed by love for her son to hear the rattling bones. That house has the most skeletons: a ghostly father weeping for his two lost daughters, a young Vietnamese mother rocking an empty cradle, Rebecca's half sister, arms held out through flames, and Bill's regret is the loudest rattler.

Across the street is my house, number 10—we'll come back to it. Look at the right upstairs window at number 8. That's Mr. Simon with his binoculars aimed at Opal Palacio's house. Mr. Simon thinks his skeleton is his father, whom I've seen marching naked down the middle of the street late at night. But the real skeleton is the memory of his mother, her greedy fingers holding him back from the knowledge of love.

Opal's closets and rooms in number 11 are full of food and music. There's barely enough room now for the starving, skinny skeleton that used to pop out at her every morning.

The great big house at the end is number 12 where Mavis Otis lives, and like I said, her skeletons are real: Papa and Mama and a lost love. No matter how much she fills the house and piles up money, she can't drive them out and she can't fill the emptiness inside herself.

Here we are back at number 10, my house. I don't have to look through these walls because I live inside them. Kids are naturally curious, but Millennium Extrasensory Evolution Kids have a need to know everything. We listen at doors, go through closets and drawers when no one else is home, and get up late at night to look out our windows. I know Hank is bulimic, and I can't believe my dad doesn't know. But then, Dad prefers not to notice anything that might upset his rose-colored view of life. If Hank let his secrets out, they would all come in a rush, and Dad would have to confront his own fear of "coming out" beyond the walls of our house. He's afraid of losing Hank and afraid of losing me. He thinks my mother may show up one day and take me away from him.

I don't know her, I don't want to know her, and I would never leave this neighborhood. Nature has endowed Millennium Extrasensory Evolution Kids with certain gifts in order to thrive. And the best places to thrive are neighborhoods just like mine. We not only see through walls, we see time pass in leaves, the colors of snow and grass, spiders sleeping, the moon reflected in a possum's eyes, and we don't mistake bats for swallows at dusk.

We hear not only what you meant to say, we hear ice melting, whales mourning, mercury rising, cocoons spinning, and we don't mistake cicadas for sirens. We feel fissures forming, salmon spawning, our legs in motion and pins drop.

We smell and taste photosynthesis, pheromones, apathy, and carcinoma, and we don't mistake anger for fear. That's the greatest difference between us and the rest of you—we know what to fear and, more important, what not to fear. We shall inherit the earth.

PERMISSIONS ACKNOWLEDGMENTS

Some chapters originally appeared in the following:
"Tuesday's Child," *River City* (Summer 2000),
"Wednesday's Child," *Sonora Review* (Spring 1983), and
subsequently in a slightly different form and under a different
title in *Vital Signs: Contemporary Fiction about Medicine,*
St. Martin's Press (Fall 1990).

Grateful acknowledgment is made to *Warner Bros. Publications
U.S. Inc.* and *Bob-A-Lew Music* for permission to reprint an
excerpt from the song lyric "Jacob's Ladder" by B. R. Hornsby
and John Hornsby. Copyright © 1986 by WB Music Corp.,
Zappo Music, Basically Gasp Music, and Bob-A-Lew Songs
(ASCAP). All rights on behalf of Zappo Music administered by
WB Music Corp. All rights reserved. Reprinted by permission of
Warner Bros. Publications U.S. Inc. and Bob-A-Lew Music.

About the Author

PAMELA DITCHOFF is a writer whose fiction, poetry, and nonfiction have appeared in numerous periodicals and anthologies. Her first novel, *The Mirror of Monsters and Prodigies,* was published by Coffee House Press. She is also the author of two teaching texts published by Interact Press. She lives in East Lansing, Michigan, and Liverpool, Nova Scotia.